"I was born old," June said.

Wasn't that always the mantra with people who were too young? Kevin mused. His eyes swept over her beautiful face. Her perfect, smooth heart-shaped face. "You don't look all that old to me."

"I could say the same about you." Her smile flashed, casting a spectrum like the northern lights. Mostly within him.

"Of course, you might need to take a little closer look at me. Sometimes your eyes play tricks on you." June stepped closer to him, raising her face up for his inspection.

Kevin doubted if he'd ever seen a complexion so flawless. Or compelling. "No, no tricks," he murmured. Other than the one his own pulse executed by vibrating faster than he could ever remember.

The grin entered her eyes and then slowly, enticingly, faded as she looked up into his face. It took her a second to find her voice.

"So, do I kiss you o

Dear Reader,

Breeze into fall with six rejuvenating romances from
Silhouette Special Edition! We are happy to feature our
READERS' RING selection, *Hard Choices* (SE#1561), by
favorite author Allison Leigh, who writes, "I wondered about
the masks people wear, such as the 'good' girl/boy vs. the 'bad'
girl/boy, and what ultimately hardens or loosens those masks.
Annie and Logan have worn masks that don't fit, and their past
actions wouldn't be considered ideal behavior. I hope readers
agree this is a thought-provoking scenario!"

We can't get enough of Pamela Toth's WINCHESTER BRIDES
miniseries as she delivers the next book, *A Winchester Homecoming*
(SE#1562). Here, a world-weary heroine comes home only to
find her former flame ready to reignite their passion. MONTANA
MAVERICKS: THE KINGSLEYS returns with Judy Duarte's
latest, *Big Sky Baby* (SE#1563). In this tale, a Kingsley cousin
comes home to find that his best friend is pregnant. All of a
sudden, he can't stop thinking of starting a family…with her!

Victoria Pade brings us an engagement of convenience and a
passion of *in*convenience, in *His Pretend Fiancée* (SE#1564),
the next book in the MANHATTAN MULTIPLES miniseries.
Don't miss *The Bride Wore Blue Jeans* (SE#1565), the last in
veteran Marie Ferrarella's miniseries, THE ALASKANS. In
this heartwarming love story, a confirmed bachelor flies to Alaska
and immediately falls for the woman least likely to marry! In
Four Days, Five Nights (SE#1566) by Christine Flynn, two
strangers are forced to face a growing attraction when their
small plane crashes in the wilds.

These moving romances will foster discussion, escape and lots
of daydreaming. Watch for more heart-thumping stories that
show the joys and complexities of a woman's world.

Happy reading!

Karen Taylor Richman,
Senior Editor

Please address questions and book requests to:
Silhouette Reader Service
U.S.: 3010 Walden Ave., P.O. Box 1325, Buffalo, NY 14269
Canadian: P.O. Box 609, Fort Erie, Ont. L2A 5X3

The Bride Wore Blue Jeans

MARIE FERRARELLA

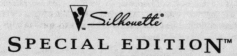

SPECIAL EDITION™

Published by Silhouette Books

America's Publisher of Contemporary Romance

To Michael,
who never gives up.

Love,
Marysia

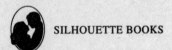 SILHOUETTE BOOKS

ISBN 0-373-24565-3

THE BRIDE WORE BLUE JEANS

Copyright © 2003 by Marie Rydzynski-Ferrarella

Visit Silhouette at www.eHarlequin.com

Printed in U.S.A.

Books by Marie Ferrarella in Miniseries

MARIE FERRARELLA

earned a master's degree in Shakespearean comedy, and, perhaps as a result, her writing is distinguished by humor and natural dialogue. This RITA® Award-winning author's goal is to entertain and to make people laugh and feel good. She has written over one hundred books for Silhouette, some under the name Marie Nicole. Her romances are beloved by fans worldwide and have been translated into Spanish, Italian, German, Russian, Polish, Japanese and Korean.

Dear Reader,

Well, here we are, at the end of the line for this miniseries. Who would have ever thought we'd come so far? The very first story of The Alaskans was inspired by a TV series I watched aeons ago, a turn-of-the-last-century tale that was set in Alaska. *Wife in the Mail* was only supposed to be a single story about a lady who wanted to find a fresh start in a pristine part of our beloved country. But while telling her story, I fell in love with the hero's best friend, Ike, the guy who ran the old-fashioned saloon in Hades. And well, he had a cousin, whose future wife had two brothers and a sister and…well, you know how it goes. I've always been a little long-winded.

But now it's time to tie up the tales with a bow by giving you Kevin and June's story. I hope you enjoy reading it half as much as I've enjoyed writing it, and if this does strike a chord or two, maybe you'll find the time and the urge to go revisit some of the other citizens of Hades. When you do, say hi for me. I miss them already.

I wish you love and happiness.

Best,

Marie Ferrarella

Chapter One

He missed them.

Kevin Quintano carefully placed the framed eight-by-ten photograph he'd been looking at for the past ten minutes back on his coffee table and sighed. He could almost hear the laughter in that photograph, taken at Jimmy's graduation from medical school. It was of the four of them. Alison, Lily, Jimmy and him.

He truly missed them.

Missed the sound of their voices, missed the good-natured bickering between his younger siblings that he'd once thought would send him up a wall. Missed life the way it used to be.

There were times when the silence became overwhelming. To get away from it, he'd turned on a radio or a television set in every room of the house, just to hear people talking, just to see images.

But the silence wasn't the worst of it. The loneliness was.

You'd think now, at thirty-seven, with no debts and more money than he knew what to do with, for the very first time in his life he'd kick back and enjoy himself.

"Damn, Kevin, you can live the high life now," Nathan had said enviously at his recent farewell party. The big, strapping black man and the other cab drivers who used to work for him had come together and thrown a party just for him.

Trouble was, Kevin mused, moving into the kitchen to prepare a lunch he had no desire to eat, he had neither wanted the high life, nor known what to do with it should he ever wind up stumbling across it.

What he wanted was the busy life. The life that barely gave him enough time to draw two breaths together in succession.

Kevin stared into the refrigerator. It was nearly empty. He'd forgotten to go grocery shopping. Again. Lily used to take care of that for him because he was always too busy to do it himself.

Too busy.

That's the way it had been ever since he'd turned seventeen and, through some creative doctoring of his birth certificate, had gotten himself placed in charge of his orphaned brother and sisters. Overnight he'd become both mother and father to three kids without the comforting benefit of having a spouse or ever having procreated.

And now, he thought, he was experiencing the empty-nest syndrome under the same set of circumstances.

Big time.

That was probably why, in a moment of weakness—because Nathan and Joe had talked him into thinking that perhaps a huge change might shake him out of his doldrums—he'd sold his taxicab service. The very same service that had seen his fledgling family through the hard times. The same service that had allowed him to put food on the table and take out a loan so that Jimmy could go to medical school and graduate as something more than a pauper with an incredible debt to repay.

It was Kevin who had shouldered the debt. And he who'd been so damn proud of his brother at graduation.

In its time, the taxicab service had also allowed him to put Alison, the baby of the family, through nursing school and to set Lily up in her very first restaurant when they'd all decided that she had an incredible gift for creating meals but no capacity for taking orders.

And where had all that loan-incurring finally gotten him?

Alone, that's where.

Alone while the rest of them, the three people who mattered most in his life, had gone off, one by one, to live in Alaska, in some godforsaken place aptly labeled Hades.

Hell.

Wandering back into the living room, Kevin dropped down into the sofa and stared blankly at a woman trying vainly to escape a horde of rampaging twelve-foot spiders. Midday programs were hellish, too.

That was where he felt he was right now. In hell. And he'd discovered something these past few weeks. It wasn't fire and brimstone that created a hell, it was bare-bones loneliness. Loneliness comprised of slick, glasslike walls that sent him sliding back to the ground no matter how quickly he tried to scale them.

He knew he should be proud of his siblings and the selflessness they'd exhibited to varying degrees. Alison had gone first, because Hades needed a nurse and she needed to get certified as a nurse-practitioner by putting time in a place like that.

Only problem was, she'd put in her heart as well and so had remained.

When Jimmy had gone to visit her, he'd lost his heart as well. Not to the region, but to April Yearling, the granddaughter of Hades's postmistress. Hades and the surrounding region badly needed another doctor and Jimmy had found his true calling.

Lily's broken engagement had brought her to the same place to recover, Alaska being the only place that could withstand the heat of her anger without frying to a crisp. Intending to stay only two weeks, Lily found solace for her wounded pride and chipped heart with Hades sheriff, Max Yearling, who just happened to be April's brother.

It was as if the Fates were conspiring to bring his family to a place that spent six months of every year in a deep freeze, cut off from civilization except by air travel.

Kevin had thought—hoped—that Alaska might be a passing phase with Lily. Lily had always been the mercurial one, the one who never invested her emotions for fear of being hurt. But this time, she apparently was sticking it out, and the last time he'd spoken to her, she'd said something about bringing real food to the residents of Hades and had her eye on opening a restaurant there. He knew the signs by now. Lily, like Alison and Jimmy before her, was settling in for good.

Unable to watch the giant spiders destroy yet another campsite and assorted campers, Kevin flipped the channel. The afternoon news looked no less disconcerting. He dropped the remote on the table, giving up.

The restlessness refused to abate.

It was this restlessness that had made him so susceptible to Nathan and Joe's suggestion about selling the cab service. He'd done it on a lark, put the business up for sale. His heart hadn't really been in it. And then that offer had come in. The one he couldn't refuse without submitting himself to a sanity hearing because it was so incredibly lucrative.

So here he was, a man of leisure who knew absolutely nothing about taking it easy except what he'd learned lately, which was that he hated it. That he wasn't cut out for it in any manner, shape or form.

Which was why he'd been searching through the Seattle classifieds this Sunday morning, looking at the section that listed businesses for sale and trying to figure out what to do with himself other than making the electric company rich by pumping electricity through every room of the empty house. The house where he and his brother and sisters had grown up in.

"What you need, boy, is a fine-looking woman to take your mind off everything." That had been Nathan's solution, delivered sagely over a mug of ale.

Fine-looking women were Nathan's solution to everything, up to and including global warming and the threat of an alien invasion. However, that wasn't his solution, Kevin thought. Not even remotely.

He got up and shut off the television set and picked up the classifieds again. Maybe there was something he'd missed the first time.

Looks had never meant anything to him. Heart did.

Heart and soul and patience. But all the women he'd known possessing those qualities had been taken long before now.

Besides, there wasn't much chance of a woman like that showing up at his door, and that would be the only way he'd run into one. He didn't believe in any of the conventional ways of "hooking up" with members of the fairer sex. That had never been his way. And now that he no longer occasionally drove a cab, there was absolutely no chance of his meeting anyone.

Kevin paused, trying to remember the last time he'd actually gone out on a date. Nothing came to him.

But dating, or finding a lifelong partner wasn't why he was looking to put his newfound fortune into another business. He just wanted to be doing something. Something productive.

Anything productive.

He'd been out of the taxicab business for exactly five days and was going stir-crazy.

The phone rang and he grabbed the receiver like a drowning man grabbing at a twig floating by him in the river.

If it was a telemarketer on the other end, he thought, this was their lucky day. He was buying, as long as buying meant he could hear the sound of another person's voice responding to his own.

"Hello?"

"Kev?"

Kevin could feel himself lighting up inside like a Christmas tree the instant he heard his sister's voice on the other end of the line.

"Lily, how are you?" He bit back the desire to ask the next question that loomed in his mind in twenty-four-foot neon letters: Are you coming home? He already knew the answer to that. Asking wasn't going to change it.

"I'm terrific, Kev. Better than terrific, I'm spectacular."

He didn't have to see her to know that she was positively glowing. So much for her throwing in the towel and deciding to move back to Seattle.

There was something else in her voice he recognized as well. "You're getting married, aren't you?"

There was a slight pause on the other end of the line. "God, but you're good. How did you—?"

A small laugh escaped him. "I've had this conversation before. Twice," he reminded her. "When Alison called to say she was marrying Luc and when Jimmy called to say he was staying on as a doctor in Hades and, oh, by the way, yes, he was getting married."

If Jimmy, a guy known to his friends as the eternal happy bachelor could succumb to the charms of a homegrown native, Kevin had known in his heart that Lily wasn't far behind. Especially when she'd called before to give him a detailed description of Max

Yearling right down to his worn, size-ten boots. It was only a matter of waiting for the shoe to finally drop, that's all.

Kevin knew he was happy for her, even as he was sad for himself. He did his best to sound cheerful. "So the sheriff makes you happy, does he?"

Lily sighed, contentment of a caliber he didn't ever recall hearing before in her voice. "The way you wouldn't believe."

Kevin felt his mouth curving in a grin. "I don't need details, Lily."

"And you're not getting any," she informed him with a laugh. "But I want you to come up here. For the wedding. It's in three weeks and I wouldn't feel as if it's official unless you're here to give me away."

He refrained from saying that no one had ever held on to her long enough to pretend that she was his to give away. Lily had been her own person from a very early age.

Yes, he thought, he really was going to miss her.

"I'd be proud to, Lily."

He heard her clear her throat. Lily hated to get sentimental. "Now I know how you feel about getting away from the business, but maybe Nathan or Joe could take over while—"

He cut her off briskly. "Not a problem. I sold the business." In response, he heard nothing but silence on the other end. Everything had happened so quickly he hadn't even had time to tell any of them that he was thinking about selling, much less that he'd signed on the dotted line and made Quintano Cabs a thing of the past. "Lily, are you there?"

He heard her take in a sharp breath. "Yes, I guess the connection just went weird for a second. I thought I heard you say—"

He didn't want to hear her say it. He couldn't exactly explain why hearing one of his siblings give voice to what he'd done would make it that much more difficult to bear, but it did. "You did. I did."

"But, Kevin, why?"

The last thing he wanted to do now was discuss what he'd impulsively done over the telephone. He needed to reconcile himself to today's wrinkle first, then think about his late business.

"Seemed like the thing to do at the time." He changed the topic. "Anyway, three weeks, eh? That's really short notice. You've got a lot to do before then."

"I know." She sighed, as if trying to brace herself for what lay ahead. "I can manage—"

He suddenly knew what to do with himself. At least, for the next three weeks. "Especially with help. I'll come up early."

"How early?"

Unless he missed his guess, he'd managed to stun Lily twice in the space of two minutes. "I'm not doing anything right now. I'll be there as soon as possible." He was already walking toward the cabinet where he kept the phonebooks stashed. "Let me book a flight and then I'll get back to you."

Still very numb, Lily murmured a half-audible "Okay."

"Great. Talk to you later. Bye."

The line went dead. Lily let the receiver drop slowly as she turned around to face the rest of her family who were gathered in the room around her. Her brother and sister were there with their spouses, as well as Max and June, who absolutely refused to be left out of anything, family oriented or otherwise. Alison and Jimmy looked at her in surprise, clearly disappointed that they didn't each get a chance to talk to Kevin on the phone.

Closest to her, Jimmy stared at the medical clinic telephone, one of the few in Hades that didn't still possess a rotary dial. He raised his eyes to hers in protest. "You hung up."

"He hung up first," Lily muttered, still staring at the receiver and feeling as if a piece of the known world had just disappeared from her life.

Max came around to face her. "Lily, what's the matter? Isn't your brother coming?"

Slowly she nodded her head. Sold, the business was sold. Gone. Wow. She would have thought that the Space Needle would have wound up on eBay for an auction before Kevin would ever even consider selling the taxicab service.

"Oh, he's coming all right." Raising her eyes, she looked at the others.

"Then what's the matter?" Max asked.

Lily's eyes met his. "Kevin just told me he's sold the business."

"He did what?" Jimmy's jaw went slack. He'd put in seven summers driving one of Kevin's cabs. It was as if a member of the family had died

Lily turned to look at him. "Sold the business." Unable to fathom it, she waved her hand vaguely in the air. "Said it seemed like the thing to do."

She looked from one face to another as if waiting for one of them to unravel the mystery for her, to make sense of the situation. Why would Kevin do that? He *loved* the business.

June Yearling lifted her slender shoulders, wondering what the big deal was all about. People sold businesses every day. She had, just recently. The one-time owner of the only auto-repair shop in over a hundred-mile radius, she'd sold the business that had been passed on to her, because it had felt like the right thing to do at the time.

"Maybe it was," she said to her brother's fiancée. "Maybe he has an itch, and selling his taxicab service is the only way he knows how to scratch it."

Lily sighed. It still didn't make any sense to her. Kevin was acting rashly, especially for Kevin. Why hadn't he discussed this with any of them? She looked at Jimmy and Alison, but they looked as mystified as she was.

Lily ran her hands up and down her arms, despite the fact that the day was warm. "But he's had that business forever."

June thought of herself, of her own feelings when she'd made up her mind to sell. "Forever's a long time. Maybe he needed something new. Maybe he got tired of having things break down on him and—" She bit her lip, realizing that she'd allowed her own experiences to intrude into her interpretation. "Sorry. They always say, stick to what you know."

Max laughed shortly, shaking his head. She might have the face of an angel, but June was the wild one in the family, especially now that April had ceased her wandering ways and returned to live in Hades. June had never made noises about moving out of state, the way over three-quarters of the adolescent population had, but she had been a restless pistol in every other way. She was always full of surprises.

"If that were the case," he said to her, "you wouldn't have sold the shop to Walter Haley and announced that you were going to make a go of the family farm."

Family farm.

It was almost a euphemism at this point. In reality, it had been abandoned land for years. They'd left it without any thought when he, Alison and June, along with their mother, had moved in with their grandmother after their father had taken off for parts unknown. The thought of making a go of the property had vaguely crossed his mind, only to be quickly discarded. The town needed a sheriff and he needed to be it. Max knew he was lucky enough to have found his true calling.

June frowned, looking down at her hands. They were scrubbed clean now, but there were still traces of dark stains on them. She'd never been one to dress up or try to compete with her sister, or any of the other girls in town, but even she had a place where she drew the line.

"I got tired of trying to get motor oil off my hands," she retorted. She looked accusingly at the older brother she secretly adored. "A woman's got a right to want to keep her hands clean."

Max gave her an innocent look. "Never said otherwise."

Concern creased Alison's fair features as she looked at her own brother. "Think Kevin's having a midlife crisis?"

Luc laughed at his wife's suggestion, shaking his head. He'd always liked Kevin. "Thirty-seven's a little young to have a midlife crisis."

June looked at him. She might be the youngest in the room, but age to her was not a brittle thing, without rounded edges or flexibility. "Seems to be just about right to me. Unless he's planning on living until he's a hundred."

Jimmy smiled, remembering the promise Alison had extracted from their brother after their father's funeral. "Kevin is planning on living forever."

"Well, then you're right," she said glibly. "Thirty-seven's too young for a midlife crisis. Maybe he just needed a change." With the bluntness of the very young, she looked at Kevin's siblings. "After all, you all picked up and left him."

It almost sounded like an accusation. Lily exchanged glances with Jimmy.

"None of us planned it that way," Alison protested for all of them.

June shrugged. She had to be getting back to work. The land wasn't going to tend itself. And she still had cows to milk and a disabled tractor to curse. "Still, that's what happened. Maybe he thinks it's time to start over."

Jimmy looked thoughtful. Maybe June had stumbled across something. "In Kevin's case, it's starting life in the first place. He's never had time for a life," he told his in-laws. "Been there for all of us and never had time to be there for himself."

June looked triumphant. "Mystery solved," she announced. "This is his time for himself."

Alison tried to keep the sad feeling at bay, but it insisted on coming. She looked at Jimmy. "Still, it feels kind of weird, knowing the taxi service is gone."

Jimmy nodded his agreement. All three of them

had taken turns putting in time at the service and driving a cab, even Lily. Driving a cab was how Alison had met Luc in the first place. Luc had come down from Hades, looking for someone to pretend to be his wife in order to cover an inadvertent white lie. He'd wound up saving Alison from a mugger and sustaining a concussion. To pay him back for his trouble, especially after she'd discovered the nursing shortage in Hades, Alison had agreed to the charade and stayed on to play the part in earnest.

Crossing to the door, June placed her hand on the latch.

"Probably no weirder than he's feeling with all of you gone." She opened the door. "Well, I've got to be getting back to work. I'll see you all later."

Max shook his head as June closed the door. He put his arms around Lily, giving her a hug to stave off the bout of guilt he saw in her eyes. "Always said June was the cheerful one in the family."

Jimmy looked after his sister-in-law thoughtfully. The last time Kevin had come up here, it had been to take part in his wedding. At twenty, June had seemed too young at the time. She wasn't too young now.

"Maybe that's what we can do to get Kevin's mind off whatever's really bothering him."

"Do?" Lily echoed. "Do what? What are you talking about?"

But Alison was already on Jimmy's wavelength. "We'll tell Kevin that June needs cheering up." She brightened immensely. "Kevin's at his best when he's dealing with someone else's problems." She looked at the others. "The man is a problem solver. He misses having to deal with all our baggage."

Lily sniffed. "We didn't come with baggage."

Jimmy gave his older sister a pointed look. "You had your own luggage store."

She laughed shortly. "And Casanova didn't?"

Max grinned as he tightened his arms around his wife-to-be. "I'm beginning to understand what Kevin did in the family. He kept the peace."

Lily got off her high horse. Turning, she brushed a kiss against her future husband's cheek.

"I'd say that gives Kevin something in common with you."

Dealing with Lily was where his people-reading skills came in handiest—and were the most challenged. "I'm not flattering myself," Max told her. "I keep the peace for any one of a number of residents here. I know better than to try to exercise control over you."

"This marriage," Jimmy announced to the others, "should work out just fine."

He ducked, but Max was quicker and caught Lily's hand as she went to throw her cell phone at him.

"Yes," Max agreed, looking at Lily meaningfully as he gently pushed her hand down again, "it should."

Lily's eyes sparkled, negating the frown she was attempting to form.

Chapter Two

Kevin slowly looked around at the groups of people milling around him at the Anchorage airport. He'd only gotten off the plane from Seattle fifteen minutes ago.

It seemed longer.

He felt a little homesick already, which was odd because Seattle had never been anything more to him than steel girders set against an almost continually misting sky.

He supposed it had to do with his all-too-common need for the familiar. He wasn't a man who suffered change well, although he wouldn't have admitted this out loud to anyone, not even one of his siblings.

The irony of it struck him as he continued to scan the interior of the airport. He might not do change well, but here he was, right smack-dab in the midst of it. Change. Change in his family structure now that they were all up here in Alaska and he was back in Seattle, and change in the very fiber of his life since he'd sold the only business he'd known for the past twenty years. Driving a cab had been his very first job. He'd started out as a driver for the company, saving and working endless hours, until he could manage, with the help of a bank loan and the money in the small trust fund his parents had left him, to buy the cab service when it was put up for sale.

Back then, it had been only a three-cab company and the venture was decidedly risky, but he felt it was the only way to assure the futures of the three people who were depending on him.

The thought added another blanket to the sorrow that threatened to smother him these days. There was no one depending on him now. Not his family, not the people who worked for him, because there *were* no people who worked for him anymore.

It felt incredibly odd, being this free.

Freedom, Kevin decided as he took yet another pass around the busy airport, was highly overrated and completely unfulfilling. At least as far as he was concerned.

Dueling with a feeling of irritability, he glanced at his watch. His plane had been late getting in. His "ride," otherwise known as the connecting private plane flight that would finally bring him to Hades, was even later. At least, he didn't see his brother or either of his sisters in the vicinity.

Maybe something had happened and they weren't coming. Maybe there'd been another cave-in at the mines and the whole town was involved in a rescue operation. It wouldn't be the first time.

He didn't see why they couldn't all just move back to Seattle.

Feeling antsy, Kevin scanned the back walls to see if he could spy a car rental counter. It was the tail end of summer, and snow hadn't come yet to cut off access to the small town his family had chosen to live in. If worse came to worst and no one showed up for him, he figured he could drive there—as long as someone handed him a map or at least pointed him in the right direction. He'd always prided himself on being able to find any place, given enough time.

Kevin supposed that made up for the fact that when it came to interacting with people, he'd always found it better just to listen rather than talk. Alison had once said that gave him a wise aura. He thought of himself as shy.

"Kevin?"

He didn't recognize the woman's voice coming from behind him. Turning around, he didn't recognize the woman, either. At least, not immediately.

His eyes washed over a petite, trim woman wearing

a work shirt rolled up at the sleeves and a pair of very worn blue jeans that had either originally belonged to someone else, or were a living testimony that she'd lost a goodly amount of weight. Kevin suspected it was the former. The young woman had hair the color of a radiant sunrise and eyes so blue they drew out the last drops of loneliness that were lingering within him. Her hair was pulled back into a single long braid, exposing a face that was kissed by the sun and was as close to heart-shaped as humanly possible.

And then it came to him.

Two years ago, when he'd last seen her, she'd been a child. Twenty years old and just finding her way into her features. Two years had obviously done a great deal to show her the right path.

She was, without benefit of makeup and with absolutely no care whatsoever, one of the loveliest young women he'd ever seen.

"June?"

Her grin was quick, like lightning that came and went in a blink. While it was there, it transformed her face from remote to warmingly friendly. Kevin felt something within him quicken.

He recalled hearing Jimmy tell him that if June Yearling liked you, you had a friend for life, someone to rely on no matter what. But by the same token, she selected the people she was close to very carefully, as if they were slivers of gold to be separated from the seductive but worthless fool's gold.

June slipped her hand into his, shaking it before he even realized that he'd offered it to her.

"Hi, they sent me to get you." She turned then, looking at the blond woman behind her. "Actually, they sent us," she amended.

June cocked her head to look at him, as if to decide whether or not he remembered them, or if reintroductions were in order.

He recognized the other woman more quickly. Sydney Kerrigan. She was the doctor's wife. The doctor who had convinced Jimmy to remain here. The one who'd originally enticed his sister to come before that.

No, he amended, that wasn't entirely right. Luc had been the one to convince Alison where her place was, and April had been the deciding factor in Jimmy's life. It had been more for love than for work that they had each remained.

Love, it seemed, made the world go around. Just not in his case.

But that boat had been one that had sailed a long time ago. Kevin knew that. He'd made his choice. It had come down to either Dorothy, or his siblings. But that had hardly been a contest. Dorothy had never stood a chance. Anyone who'd asked him to choose between them and his family wasn't anyone he wanted to spend the rest of his life with.

It just got lonely sometimes, that's all. Especially now with so much of life behind him.

The young woman in front of him, he thought, had the whole world before her.

He wondered why she hadn't left the confines of her Alaskan "prison" the way so many of her age had, according to Jimmy. He was the one who'd told him about the penchant most Alaskan teenagers had for fleeing the area the moment they were old enough.

Jimmy's own wife, April, June's sister, had shot out of the region like a bat out of hell the moment she'd turned eighteen. Only her grandmother's illness had brought her back. Temporarily, she'd thought. She was still here.

As for him, Kevin couldn't help wondering what the allure was, what kind of magical pull the region exercised over people like April, Max and June. Why were they still here when there was so much more to be had in the lower forty-nine?

"Jimmy and Alison couldn't get away," June was explaining. "The vaccine they'd been waiting for came in. They needed to get inoculations underway immediately."

At least, that was what Jimmy had told her. She still thought the excuse was a little fishy, but she'd needed a break anyway. If it wasn't for the fact that she hated accepting defeat in any shape or size, she would have begun rethinking the wisdom of her change in occupation. Farming was not the closest thing to her heart, but making a go of the family farm had become a matter of honor to her.

Getting in front of Sydney, June reached for Kevin's suitcase. "And Lily's busy getting ready."

The woman looked as solid as a spring breeze. He placed his hand over the handle, stopping her from picking up the luggage. "Ready for what, the wedding?"

"You," Sydney told him over June's head.

"Me?" That didn't make any sense. Why would Lily be fussing over his arrival? "I've seen her first thing in the morning, stumbling down the stairs wearing an old pair of men's pajamas and looking like hell on an off day. There's no need to get ready for me."

An enigmatic smile played on Sydney's, his pilot's, lips. "It's a little more complicated than that," Sydney told him. "But I'm sworn to secrecy." Playfully she held up a hand to stop any further exchange on the subject. "Sorry, you won't get any more out of me."

"Fair enough," he allowed, then looked at his future sister-in-law. She made another attempt to take the case from him. "I can carry my own suitcase, June. I'm not that old yet."

June raised her hand, visually surrendering her claim to the large piece of carry-on luggage. The man traveled light, she thought. An admirable quality. Of course, if this had been winter, it would have also been a foolish one, she silently added.

"You're not old at all," she countered. Shrugging,

she slipped her capable hands into the front pockets of her jeans. "I'm just used to doing, that's all."

The single word hung out there like a forgotten T-shirt on a clothesline. "Doing?"

"Everything," June said all inclusively. Accustomed to being challenged, she raised her chin. "Just because I'm a female doesn't mean I can't hold my own. Better than my own," she amended.

Kevin exchanged glances with Sydney. The latter merely looked amused. He certainly hadn't meant to give any offense.

"That was never under debate," he told June. "But I like pulling my own weight, too."

Sydney shook her head. This might not go as well as the others were hoping. As for herself, she believed in letting nature take its course. If something was meant to be, it would be. She was living proof of that, having come out to marry a man who had won her heart through his letters, and wound up marrying his brother instead.

"Well, when you're both finished pulling on the same weight," Sydney informed Kevin, "the plane's over this way."

Turning, she led the way out of the airport. Kevin gestured June on ahead of him. With a tolerant sigh, the latter turned on the heel of her boot and followed Sydney. Her long, shiny blond braid swung behind her and then marked time with her gait before it finally settled into place.

Kevin found himself watching, mesmerized for a brief moment. Coming to, he smiled and shook his head as he hurried to catch up to the two women. You would have thought he was an adolescent, he mused, mildly upbraiding himself.

Kevin stared out the small window. Below him the world had arranged itself in a carpet of green with ribbons of blue cutting through it here and there. In the distance, and getting taller, was a mountain range. The rattle of the plane didn't detract from the experience. It just made it more intimate.

They hit an air pocket and the plane shuddered. Sydney glanced over her shoulder to see if her passenger was all right. When Alison's brother had come out the last time, Shayne had been the one who'd piloted him back and forth.

She was pleased to see that Kevin was intent on studying the landscape instead of grasping onto the seat rests for dear life.

"You don't turn green like a lot of other people flying in this little plane." Her tone was approving.

Kevin leaned forward in his seat in order to hear Sydney better. "I trust the pilot. Besides, I like to fly. I'm licensed to fly a twin engine."

She'd loved flying from the first time she'd had her hands on the throttle. "Maybe you'd like to take her up while you're here."

He'd like that, he thought. But he had a very healthy

respect for other people's property and this plane was one that was used by Shayne to fly medical supplies into Hades and patients to Anchorage Memorial when they needed serious surgery.

"Maybe," Kevin said.

Sydney detoured, guiding the plane around a cloud formation. He found himself admiring her form. "Are you still the only pilot in and out of Hades? Besides your husband," he qualified. Shayne, he recalled, had been the one to originally teach Sydney how to fly. Although grudgingly done, that had turned out to be a good thing for him, since she'd been the one who had to fly Shayne into Anchorage when he'd had appendicitis.

She'd gotten so used to the addition it took her a second to grasp the question. Her world had become small enough that it was easy to forget that everyone wasn't privy to what went on in Hades.

"No, Mr. Kellogg's son decided that he was going to expand his produce flights and operate out of Hades. That brings our total of planes up to two, but we certainly need more," Sydney confided. "We've been doing a lot of growing since you were here last."

He looked out the window. The plane was approaching Hades. It certainly didn't appear as if the town, with its population of barely five hundred, was growing at all. From here, it still looked like a small, colorful dot on the ground. Hardly big enough to occupy even a tiny corner of a city like Seattle.

Sitting next to him, June looked at him knowingly. She could all but read the thoughts forming in his head. "Not exactly a thriving metropolis yet," she agreed. "But we're getting there. Slowly."

He shifted back into his seat. "You still run the only mechanic shop in town?"

"No." Despite her excuse to her brother, she had to admit that there were times she missed the shop. Missed puzzling over what was wrong with an engine, or how to resurrect a car that seemed to be on its last legs. Missed the triumphant feeling when it all finally came together. "Walter runs it now."

"Walter?" He tried to recall if any of his siblings had mentioned a Walter. He made the natural leap. "Is that your husband?"

Kevin glanced at her hand. It was barren of jewelry, just as it had been two years ago. But then, she didn't strike him as the type to have any use for a ring as a symbol of her commitment.

Thinking of the tall, gawky man who had, until recently, tried to convince her that they were meant to be together, June nearly choked. "Hardly. I sold him the shop a few months ago."

Kevin recalled his surprise when he'd learned that she owned a shop like that in the first place. But she had seemed very capable at the kind of work she did and as knowledgeable as any of the mechanics he'd employed at the taxi service over the years. More.

He'd had the impression, the last time he'd been here, that she was going to work on cars forever.

"Why did you sell it? I thought you liked fixing cars."

"I did." June shrugged. She had never liked explaining herself. She liked explaining her feelings even less. "Felt like it. Seemed like the thing to do at the time."

The exact words he'd used to explain the situation to Lily. And to himself, Kevin thought. The coincidence made him smile. Maybe he had more in common with this fledgling woman than he thought.

"Me, too."

One corner of June's mouth rose in a half smile. "Yeah, I know. You sold your taxi service."

She saw that he looked surprised that she knew. Obviously, the man had no inkling of what life was like in a small town. Even a small town that was spread out like Hades was. Any kind of news spread faster than Biblical locusts let loose over Egypt.

June inclined her head toward him so that he could hear her over the roar of the engine.

"I was there when Lily found out." She still got a kick out of it. "You could have knocked all of them over with a feather." In a way, she figured it gave them something in common. "Kind of like when I told Max I'd sold the shop to Walter." She sat back again. "I guess people have an image of you and they don't feel comfortable changing it."

Kevin looked at her. She was talking as if she was settled in her ways, on her way to middle age. There was only one of them like that in the plane.

"You're too young to sustain an image yet," he told her. "Me, I'm a different story."

There was that grin again. This time, the lightning came a little closer, singeing a little skin. He wondered if the altitude was getting to him.

"Right." June nodded her head sagely, a deadpan expression on her lips. "Because you're an old man. Just a little younger than the hills, right?"

Maybe he'd said too much already. Kevin began to back away. "Well, when you put it that way—"

June cocked her head, studying him. She knew he was Lily's older brother, but there were no signs of age. He looked no different than Max or Jimmy to her. If she had to make a judgment, she would have said he wasn't even as old as Sydney's husband, although she vaguely recalled hearing that he was.

"Just how old do you feel?" she asked.

Her eyes were boring into him, and he blinked to keep from being drawn into the deep light blue pools. "Too old," was all he'd volunteer.

He wasn't vain about his age. It was a matter of public record and June could have asked any of his siblings to find out that he was thirty-seven. Thirty-seven when he didn't even remember ever being twenty-five. How had that happened?

"We're going to have to do something about that,"

June decided. "Hades has a way of equalizing things, making everyone feel more or less the same. The young seem older than their years, the old seem younger. My grandmother and I are the same age, really." Everyone knew that Ursula Hatcher, the town's postmistress, was a hellion, given to kicking up her heels and certainly not above taking a lover when the mood hit her. She'd already buried several husbands and had her cap currently set for a man named Yuri, a former miner.

June smiled at him. It was a soft, easy expression that made her seem somehow softer. "That definitely puts us at the same age, old man."

He laughed, but that was the way he felt at times, like an old man. Old without ever having had the luxury of being young. He didn't even remember going through the years. They had just gone of their own volition, while he'd been busy working.

He missed that, he thought, missed being young. Thinking young.

But there was something about June's eyes that made him feel younger.

Feel young.

Watch it, Quintano, that's one of the first signs of being an old man, having a young woman make you feel like a teenager again.

He shook off the mood before he said something he regretted. "So, what other changes have there been besides you selling the shop and becoming a woman of leisure?''

June was quick to set him straight. "I'm hardly that. I'm working the family farm, now.''

Something else that was news, he thought. "I didn't know the family had a farm.''

"We did. We do. It belonged to my mother and father.'' She didn't want to launch into a long explanation. "But we left it when he left us.''

This story he was familiar with. Jimmy had told him. Wayne Yearling had had a wanderlust that was legendary. Somehow, it had allowed him to remain in Hades longer than anyone who knew him would have thought possible. But he'd finally succumbed to its call when June had been very young.

She'd grown up without a father. Kevin knew that Max wasn't that much older than she was. Max hadn't been able to step in for June the way he had with his own siblings, Kevin thought.

His heart went out to her. "I guess that gives us all something in common.''

She knew his story, too, because it was Lily's, as well. "Your father didn't leave you,'' she pointed out. "He died.''

"Sometimes it amounted to the same thing.'' The loneliness that was the end result was still the same. So was the day-to-day struggle for survival.

But she shook her head stubbornly. "Your father didn't have a choice—mine did.''

That was where they disagreed. ''Mine gave up the will to live when my mother died. He didn't seem to realize that there were more people than just him affected by her death. Or that those same people would be affected by his if he died. He chose to die.''

His own words echoed back at him. Kevin stopped abruptly and looked at her in surprise. He hadn't said that out loud to anyone. Ever. Even though it had lingered on his mind all these years. He'd been too busy making things right for the others to deal with his own feelings on the matter.

Well, he wasn't too busy now. Obviously.

Embarrassed, Kevin laughed shortly. ''I've never said that to anyone before.''

June pretended not to notice his discomfort. Her tone was glib. ''Alaska has a way of drawing confessions out of people. Gives you that kind of intimate feeling when you're around people. Makes you feel like you're all friends.''

That was one explanation, he supposed. And now that he considered it, it was the most logical. In any event, it was the one he chose to accept.

''Coming in for a landing,'' Sydney announced from the front seat, breaking into his thoughts.

Kevin looked at June and wondered if that was strictly true. It didn't feel as if he was landing at all. It felt like he was still flying.

Chapter Three

"So, what do you think?"

Trying to contain her excitement, Lily gestured out toward the wide expanse of terrain where she had decided her restaurant would stand. Building would begin after she and Max returned from their honeymoon. Unable to wait to show it off to Kevin, she'd brought him here immediately after June had delivered him to the house. They'd only stopped long enough to swing by the medical clinic so that he could quickly say hello to Alison and Jimmy. They were just closing up after an extralong day. With Max in tow, Lily had whisked her brother here with all the unsuppressed enthusiasm of a child unwrapping a long-anticipated gift on Christmas morning.

She looked at Kevin, holding her breath.

Kevin was far more taken with Lily's joy than he was with the future site of Hades's first official restaurant. She was fairly dancing from foot to foot.

"What I think is that I've never seen you this excited before."

"I don't think I ever have been." She grinned broadly as Max, standing behind her, threaded his arms around her waist.

They looked like a set, Kevin thought. As if they'd always been meant to be together.

"Maybe it's the land, or the people." Tilting her head, she cast a glance at the broad-shouldered sheriff at her back.

"Or maybe the fact that you don't sleep properly," Kevin said glibly. This giddiness was really unlike Lily. He glanced around. Daylight was permeating everything. Kevin looked at his watch. It was past seven. "When does it get dark around here?"

"It doesn't." It had taken her some getting used to. Now she didn't think she could revert to conventional days and nights easily. "At least, not this time of year. Not so you'd really notice. Sun goes down at around ten, comes up at three."

Kevin frowned. "And you find this appealing?"

"Hey, lots of daylight makes you happy," Lily told him.

Max leaned his head down. "Lots of darkness

makes you something else,'' he whispered against her hair.

But Kevin heard him. "Depressed comes to mind." The words had popped out almost of their own volition.

"Not if you have the right company." And then she frowned as she turned and looked at her older brother. "Kev, is anything wrong? I'm sensing some very unhappy vibes coming from you."

That settled it. She had definitely changed since she'd come up here. The old Lily never even had the word *vibes* in her vocabulary. He almost laughed out loud, catching himself at the last moment.

"Since when do you sound like a hippie?"

Lily waved her hand at the question. Something was definitely up with her older brother and she was concerned. "That has nothing to do with it. Kev, have you been feeling all right?"

He wasn't policing himself, Kevin thought, annoyed. There was no excuse for saying things that might bring his sister down. It wasn't fair. Lily looked as if she was finally happy for what might be the first time in her life and he had no right to rain on her parade.

Or cast a shadow as it were, he thought whimsically, glancing up at the sky.

The sun gave no indication that it was going to set, or ever had set. It could have been ten in the morning instead of well into the evening.

He forced himself to brighten visibly. "I'm feeling great." His eyes shifted to Max. "Someone is finally going to tame that tongue of yours."

A playful look entered Lily's eyes. "Someone is going to try," she corrected.

Kevin grinned at his brother-in-law. "Max, I don't think you know what you're getting into."

Max brushed a kiss against the top of Lily's head. "I once faced down a bear in a trap. I know exactly what I'm up against."

"Flattery like that is liable to turn a girl's head," Lily said wryly.

There was no use in pretending that she took offense; she felt far too happy to try to keep up a charade. Her whole family was here with her and it looked as if her whole future was finally in front of her. What was there not to be happy about?

She looked at her brother pointedly. "You didn't tell me, what do you think of it?"

The future restaurant was to stand overlooking the winding river below and the mountains in the distance. Right now, there was a velvety green carpet as far as the eye could see.

"I think it needs walls."

She gave him a little shove. "I mean the location." He knew exactly what she meant, she thought. "Look at that view, Kev." Her voice took on almost a reverent tone. "Isn't it gorgeous?"

"Breathtaking," he agreed. There was no denying that. But what would that same view look like, buried in snow? He bit back the urge to ask. Instead, he smiled at his sister. "Just like the look in your eyes." Impulsively he hugged her. "I'm happy for you, Lily." He looked at Max and Jimmy, who'd just joined them. "For all of you."

His comment sounded so exclusionary. As if they were on two sides of a fence and they were happy, while he wasn't, Lily thought. It had a very familiar ring to it. This was just the way she'd felt when she first came up here, running away from heartache without realizing that she'd wound up running to something.

An idea came to her. Lily looked up at her main reason for smiling these days. "Max, don't you think we should be getting ready?"

Max had no idea what she was talking about, but he played along gamely. "Ready? Are you sure it's supposed to be now?"

Max really was her soul mate, she thought and she dearly loved him for that and a million other things. "I'm sure." She looked at her older brother. "We're taking you to the Salty." She could see that Kevin was going to beg off. But being around people was just what he needed right now. Especially if she could orchestrate a few things. "It's tradition, you know. Whenever anyone comes to visit for more than a week, he has to have a party in his honor at the Salty."

"I came up for Jimmy's wedding," Kevin reminded her. "There wasn't any party at the Salty then."

Undaunted, Lily pressed on. "You came up for the ceremony and flew back right after it was over. There wasn't *time* for a party. But there is now." She gave him her most beguiling smile. "This way, we can really show you off."

He didn't want to be shown off. He wanted to take a quick shower and kick back for the evening. Maybe just bask in being in the same area as the rest of his family.

"I'm kind of tired, Lily."

Lily wasn't about to let him back away. She threaded her arms through his.

"No excuses, big brother. You wouldn't want to buck tradition, would you? It's bad luck. The miners are a very superstitious bunch. They wouldn't take it kindly if you turned your back on tradition."

Kevin sighed. "Wouldn't want to annoy the miners," he murmured. Maybe it wouldn't be too bad. "Who'll be there?"

"Everyone," Max told him. "There isn't enough room inside for everyone at the same time. But it's still warm enough for them to mill around outside."

They all knew that temperature here was a temperamental thing. It was August, but even if the sun didn't go down as it should, the temperature did at times, dropping down into the mid-forties without warning.

Despite the town's sudden growth spurt and new enterprises, the Salty Saloon still held the title as the favorite gathering place for the residents of Hades and its outlying regions. Owned by Ike Le Blanc and his cousin, Jean Luc, Alison's husband, it had been the beginning of the two cousins' business venture. Its success was indirectly responsible for their eventually buying the general store, restoring the town's defunct movie theater, beginning renovations on the town's one hotel and, now, investing in Lily's proposed restaurant.

Her mind racing with details she needed to take care of, primarily cornering Ike to let him know what she was up to and having Luc spread the word around town about the party, Lily quickly brushed a kiss against Kevin's cheek. ''Jimmy'll drop you off at the house and then I'll come for you in half an hour or so.''

Kevin's eyebrows drew together. Why couldn't they just proceed on to the saloon and be done with it?

But he knew better than to ask Lily for an explanation. She'd always had her own unique way of doing things and hated being questioned. Besides, he welcomed the few minutes to himself so that he could work on his enthusiasm about this so-called party in his honor. While he was happy to see everyone, the nagging thought that this was only temporary, that all too soon he'd be returning home alone after Lily's wedding, adhered to him like a slow-moving slug leeching at his happiness. He had to work his way through that before he went to the Salty.

He nodded at her compliantly. "Whatever you say, Lily."

"See?" She turned her face up to Max. "That's how it's done."

Max merely grinned as he took her hand and walked back to their vehicle.

Kevin envied them their happiness, even as he was glad for them.

There was an entire wall of people in every direction. Noise assaulted him as voices mixed with music. The smell of alcohol and smoke was everywhere. Kevin turned to the woman who had been sent to fetch him when Lily failed to turn up as promised.

"Are you sure this isn't a fire hazard?"

June grinned and shook her head as she elbowed her way in, cutting a path for him as well. "Most of the volunteer fire fighters are in here already." She raised her voice as the din went up a notch. "They don't seem to have any objections."

He had no idea who the firefighters were, but the mellow, tolerant mood that generally permeated the crowd was very apparent.

"That's because most of them are probably feeling no pain," he guessed.

June looked at him. Was that a judgmental tone? Because of the noise, she couldn't quite tell. She tried to recall if she'd ever seen him with a drink in his hand, other than toasting Jimmy at his wedding. She couldn't remember. The details of the last wedding were blurry, except for the fact that she'd thought he was one of the best-looking men she'd ever seen. With his jet-black hair, worn a bit long, his piercing green eyes and high cheekbones, he looked like Jimmy, only better.

"You don't drink?" she asked.

Right about now, he thought, a drink sounded like a pretty good thing to him. "I never said that."

"Then follow me." Taking his hand, she began to weave her way through the sea of bodies to the bar. "What's your pleasure?" she tossed over her shoulder.

The words were eaten up by the din. He raised his voice. "What?"

June stopped. Turning, she leaned in to him. Her hair, worn loose tonight even though she hadn't changed her clothes from earlier today, brushed against his face. "What's your pleasure?" she repeated.

You.

The silent response caught Kevin completely by surprise. Where the hell had that come from? He didn't think about her in those terms. In comparison to him, she was a child, for heaven's sakes. Why had he even *thought* that?

Simultaneously clearing his mind and his throat, Kevin said, "Scotch and soda," a tad too loudly.

She nodded. Her hair seemed to shimmy as it flowed about her shoulders. Kevin stifled the urge to thread his fingers through the strands and push them away from her face.

June was still holding on to his hand. He shoved the other one into his pocket to stay on the safe side.

"Sounds simple enough," she acknowledged.

Reaching the bar, she elbowed her way in and met with resistance. The man to her right wasn't budging. Tall and muscular, he was taking up more than his allotted share and laughed when she tried to get him to move. June frowned, annoyed.

"Hey, Haggerty, leave a little room for the guest of honor," she told him.

The man grinned down at her. "I'd rather leave just enough room for you, June. Say, about this much?" Holding his hands apart, he indicated the tiny pocket of area right before his torso.

Taking a step forward, Kevin found his way impeded by her hand as she waved him back. He saw June's profile become rigid. "Only if you want to sing soprano, Haggerty."

The man's grin only broadened as he struck a

cocky stance. "Oh, a few minutes with me, June, and I could have you singing another tune."

All the protective instincts he'd developed over the years galvanized in a single movement. "The lady asked you to move." Ignoring the glare June tossed his way, Kevin stepped in front of her. "I suggest you do that while you're still able to do so on your own power."

Haggerty's grin hardened a little. The man's eyes swept over him, looking him up and down. Kevin had no idea what conclusion was reached, only that he wasn't about to back down.

And then Haggerty snorted. "Bad luck to punch out the guest of honor on his first night in Hades." He drained his mug, then set it down on the counter with a slam. "Guess I'll have to wait on that."

Kevin didn't look away. "Guess so."

And suddenly Ike was on the other side of the counter, breaking up the tension with his easy voice. "On the house, Haggerty." He placed a tall glass of stout beer before the miner. "As long as you drink it over there." He pointed to a pocket of space at the far end of the saloon.

Haggerty's eyes lowered to the drink. When he raised them again, his expression could almost be called amiable. He picked up the glass. "I never said no to anything free."

Ike watched him until Haggerty was well out of earshot, then turned his attention to the two people directly before him. He wiped away a smudge on the bar. "What'll it be?"

"Scotch and soda," Kevin told him.

Reaching under the bar, Ike brought out the good stuff and began to pour. "Goes without saying that yours is free, too, Kevin." He pushed the glass toward his guest. "And a bit of advice to go with it. Next time, pick on someone your own size," he cautioned, "not a gorilla."

Kevin lifted the chunky glass in his hand. "He was bothering June."

June squared her shoulders. At five-one, she was the shortest in her family, as well as the youngest, and took offense easily because of both. "I can handle myself."

He wasn't about to argue with her. "Always nice to have backup."

Ike grinned and leaned over the bar, as if to impart some deep wisdom.

"Listen to the man, darlin'. There's strength in numbers." He glanced over to the man who was standing nursing his beer, watching them even as he was talking to someone at his side. "To my recollection, Ben Haggerty's not a mean drunk, but there's always a first time."

She shrugged, picking up the tall, foamy mug that Ike placed before her. "Worse comes to worst, I can have Max arrest him."

"Won't do you much good if it's after the fact,

darlin'," Ike commented. Someone at the far end of the bar raised his hand and called his name, though the latter melted into the din before it reached him. "Well, I'm off." He paused to nod at the glass in Kevin's hand. "Let me know when you need another." With that he moved to the other end of the bar.

Taking a long sip, Kevin looked over toward where Haggerty had gone. The man was no longer looking at them. "He give you trouble before?" Kevin wanted to know.

June took a long swig of her beer, then wiped away the foam from her upper lip. "Haggerty?" Kevin nodded in response and she shrugged. "No more than some of the others."

"The others?" Just how many men came on to Max's sister?

She hadn't given it much thought. She did now as she considered his question. "The other men." Despite the sparse lighting in the saloon, she could almost see the thoughts as they formed in Kevin's eyes. She wasn't sure if she should be insulted or touched. She settled for giving him an explanation. "Kevin, the men outnumber the women in Hades about seven to one and the winter nights out here do get lonely." She shrugged again. "Sometimes the men get a little pushy, but we've never had anyone assaulting a woman if that's what you're thinking. It's not that kind of a place."

She was young and innocent, he thought. Too bad the world wasn't that way. "Every place is that kind of a place."

She shook her head, amused, as she took another long sip. "Spoken like a man from the big city."

"No, spoken like a man who's been around, who knows that human nature isn't always as kind as we'd like it to be."

There was more, but it wasn't his place to tell her about Alison, about the way a trusted family friend had, under the guise of comforting her over her father's death, gone too far and scarred her so much as a young woman that it became almost impossible for her to ever be intimate with a man. That had it not been for Luc and his overwhelming gentleness, his sister might still be alone and hurting. It would have proved his point, but he had no intentions of revealing Alison's personal business to do it.

Finishing her beer, she set her glass down on the bar and then looked at him. A slight frown played on her lips. "Why do you do that?"

He didn't follow her. "Do what?"

Her brow furrowed with impatience. "Why do you talk as if you're an old man?"

He wasn't aware that was what he was doing, only that he was trying to make her a little less trusting. Better safe than sorry. "Well—"

"You're not, remember? I thought we settled that on the plane." She cut him off before he could offer an explanation. She didn't want one, all she wanted was for him to realize that he was still in the prime of his life.

He looked around. It was hard to judge how old most of the men in the area were. But he felt it safe to venture that they were closer to his age than to hers. "Maybe not if you consider the men in the bar." And then he looked pointedly at her. Funny, she made him feel old and young at the same time. But chronology was chronology. "But I am, in comparison to you."

She was very, very tired of being thought of as the baby in the bunch. She'd already run her own business and sold it at a profit and was now engaged in a second career. What did it take to get through to these people that she was a grown woman?

"I'm not a child."

He smiled at her. "I didn't say that."

She didn't care for the indulgence she saw in his eyes. She didn't like being humored or patronized, only acknowledged. "And I can take care of myself."

He nodded. "You already said that."

Annoyed, she blew out a breath, trying not to lose her temper. "So, what is there left to say?"

She reminded him a great deal of his sisters when they were being particularly stubborn. "Anything you want."

Somehow, through the ebbing and flowing of the crowd, they'd managed to be moved toward the door again. She took a deep breath of the outside air that had found its way into the establishment and calmed down a little. "All right, why are you so sad?"

He could only shake his head. "You don't mince words, do you?"

She knew she was outspoken and made no apologies for it. "We live life at a different pace up here. We don't move fast, but we don't miss an opportunity to say what we mean, either. We've got earthquakes, avalanches and cabin fever, and there might not be another chance, so we don't pass them up when they come." She fixed him with a penetrating look. "And you're avoiding the question. Why are you so sad?"

When she looked at him like that, he found he had trouble focusing his thoughts. "I'm not sad."

"Now you're lying," she said with equal bluntness. June shrugged. "That's okay, you don't have to answer my question. To you, I'm just a nosy stranger."

He didn't want her to think that was the way he saw her. Or that he was deliberately shutting her out. June was family, even if just extended, and family was the most important thing in the world to him. It always had been. "My whole family's up here. I miss them."

The answer was simple from where she stood. "Then stay."

She was very, very young, wasn't she? "Things are more complicated than that."

She decided she liked him. Really liked him. And as such, she decided that he needed her help. The man had to lighten up just a little or he really was going to become old before his time.

She placed a hand on his shoulder, commanding his undivided attention. "Things only get as complicated as you let them, Kevin."

Chapter Four

June paused for a moment, letting her hand drop to her side, as if suddenly aware of crossing some personal line that needed to remain uncrossed. "You have a woman back in Seattle?"

"What?" Kevin was thunderstruck by the question.

Amusement curved her mouth. "A woman. A female companion. A softer version of you," she added when he made no response. "Do you have one of those back in Seattle?"

He had no idea why he had to keep blocking the urge to touch her. "No, what makes you ask?"

She would have thought that was obvious. Kevin

was looking at her oddly. Did he think she was interested in him? It certainly wasn't meant to be a personal question on her part.

"Well, that's the only complicating factor I can think of. You sold your business. You just said that everyone you care about is up here." She connected the dots for him. "That means that you're perfectly fancy-free if you want to be."

Oh, when had life ever been that easy for him? He couldn't think back that far. "You're twenty-two, aren't you?"

Because he was Lily and Jimmy's brother, she fought her natural tendency to take offense. Instead, she kept her voice calm, even. "That has nothing to do with it. I was born old."

Wasn't that always the mantra with people who were too young? he mused. His eyes swept over her face. Her perfect, smooth, heart-shaped face. "You don't look all that old to me."

"I could say the same about you." Her smile flashed, casting a spectrum like the northern lights. Mostly within him. "Of course you might need to take a little closer look at me. It's daylight out here, but your eyes can still play tricks on you." As if to underscore her point, June stepped closer to him, raising her face up for his inspection.

He doubted if he'd ever seen a complexion so flawless. Or compelling. The woman could have easily done commercials for soap.

"No, no tricks," he murmured. Other than the one his own pulse was executing by vibrating faster than he could ever remember it having done before. "You still look as if the dew hasn't come off your life."

There it was again, that unintentional patronizing attitude. "You'd be surprised, 'old man'." The grin entered her eyes and then slowly, enticingly, faded as she looked up into his face. From out of nowhere came the feeling that everything had stood still and was holding its breath within her. It took her a second to find her voice, another to dig up her bravado. "So, do I kiss you, or do you kiss me?"

He suddenly couldn't think of anything he wanted more than to do just that. To kiss her, to feel her lips against his.

But that would be as wrong as wrong could be.

He smiled for her benefit. "Neither. If I kissed you, I'd be robbing the cradle. If you kissed me, there'd be a riot scene." He nodded toward the men standing just inside the Salty, many of whom were looking at them and trying hard to appear as if they weren't.

The stillness within her left, to be replaced by the pounding of her heart as it tried to come to terms with anticipation and something that looked as if it wasn't going to be.

"Afraid?" June challenged. She tossed her hair behind her shoulder in a movement that Kevin found impossibly sexy. "I would have never pegged you for being afraid of trying something new." She turned neatly on her heel, heading for the entrance, her voice incredibly nonchalant. "Your loss."

Yes, he thought with a deep pang, his loss. But you couldn't miss what you'd never had, right? And he had a very odd feeling that kissing June would make him acutely aware of all that he had missed in his life. And would continue missing.

This way was better.

So he watched her thread her way back into the Salty and then entered himself, going in search of a familiar face to talk to.

Lily stepped away from the window and frowned deeply. "Well, that didn't exactly go brilliantly," she muttered, acutely disappointed. She'd been watching Kevin and June since the moment of their arrival, waiting for the sparks to come. That they hadn't left an abysmal feeling in the pit of her stomach. She wanted Kevin to be happy, the way she was happy. And since love had done it for her, she felt it was only fair to assume that it would do it for him as well. It was time her brother found a little happiness. He'd been in charge of theirs all these years.

Max looked down at the surface of his beer, as if contemplating a deep philosophy. He took a sip, then raised his eyes to Lily's face.

"Wars aren't won and lost on the first encounter, Lil, or even the second. This kind of thing takes a while. Don't give up."

"A while," she echoed with a deep sigh. "How long a while? The North and South went to fight the Civil War over the weekend and that lasted four years," she lamented. The most impatient in the family, she always wanted things to happen yesterday.

Max understood where she was coming from and why she felt the way she did. He'd harbored the same feelings about June, worried that his little sister was more interested in resurrecting defunct engines than having a home and family. But unlike Lily, he knew the worth of patience and exercised it every day.

"There've been records of wars ending in under a month," he told her. She looked at him, petulant. He kissed her temple, loving her more. "I've spent a lot of time studying people. Not much else to do up here when you're isolated from the rest of the world," he qualified. "Your brother's been in a deep freeze for the past twenty years, Lily. Give him time. Give them both time. June hasn't exactly had it easy herself. It's going to take a while for them to realize that they just might be the best thing for each other. Or not," he threw in, then laughed as Lily's eyebrows rose so high they almost disappeared into her hairline.

She looked at him, appalled. "How can you say that? They're perfect for each other."

"*You* think they're perfect for each other," he pointed out. "They may have other ideas."

She frowned as she looked after her older brother.

He was almost half a room away from June. This was not going well.

"Then they're wrong." When she heard Jimmy laugh directly behind her, she swung around, immediately ready to take umbrage.

But Jimmy was looking at Max. "Better get used to that, Max. Lily's a control freak who always has to be right." Lily shot him a dark look. "Well, you are, you know."

Before Lily could retort, Max slipped his arm around her waist, pulling her even closer to him than the allotted space already warranted. "We have ways of dealing with control freaks around here."

"Tell me more." Lily forgot all about putting her brother in his place. Or trying to create a place for Kevin. Any words she might have spared melted as Max kissed her.

"Get a room, you two," Jimmy hooted.

"Got one upstairs," Ike volunteered, picking up a handful of mugs from the table behind them. "You're welcome to it."

"I think you might be needing it for a few other people," Max commented as he looked around. Here and there were the faces of men who had started wetting their whistles and lubricating themselves hours before the gathering had been labeled a party at the last minute. "Looks like some of these guys have already come close to filling their hollow legs." Max took Lily's hand in his. "Let's go talk to your other brother and see if we can get him to unwind a little."

She loved him for things like that, Lily thought, following Max. And for a whole lot more.

He'd watched her for most of the evening. In a room so crowded that air had to take a ticket in order to work its way in, Kevin found that he'd still been able to zero in on her.

June had blond hair like her sister, but April's was short and curly, while hers was long and straight and so light it looked like spun moonlight.

He doubted if he'd ever seen a woman so beautiful.

He'd thought that before, he realized.

Kevin looked accusingly down at the glass in his hand. He felt intoxicated, but that wasn't possible unless Ike had slipped something into his drink. He'd been nursing the same Scotch and soda, his second, for the past hour and a half. He held his liquor a lot better than that.

Still, every time he looked up and saw June, something strange began going on in his chest, and in his gut. Both felt as if they were tightening.

Maybe it was the lack of air.

Maybe not.

Though the room was echoing with unharnessed noise, he could have sworn he'd heard June laugh just then. He wondered who that was she was talking to. Over the course of the evening, there had been an endless parade of men seeking out her attention, some boisterous, some whispering things into her ear.

All of them appearing to be far more familiar with her than he was.

Which just made sense. But he didn't have much use for sense tonight.

He knew what was eating at him. He hadn't kissed her when the opportunity had presented itself. Just something else he was going to have to live with.

He'd had his chance and he'd turned it down.

No, that wasn't strictly true. The chance had all but been shoved into his face. Ever since he could recall, he hadn't been the type to be led around by his nose. If he kissed someone it was because he wanted to, not because someone had dared him to do it.

Trouble was, he really wanted to kiss her.

When was the last time he'd kissed any woman?

Damn it, it had been far too long. He was on vacation, he argued silently. Nothing that happened in these three weeks was going to matter in a month. In three weeks, he would go back to being himself: steadfast, dependable, honorable to a fault. And living a life that was just this side of boring.

But this was the end of the world as far as a lot of people were concerned. What a man did here could be completely out of character and still not count in the long run.

He took another long drag from his glass, letting the Scotch snake its way through his system.

For all he knew, Alaska could just be some strange dream, a product of some hermit's overactive imagination. That made what a man did here inconsequential.

Damn it, he was babbling to himself. Now he knew he'd had too much to drink, even if he'd been able to consume three times this amount and not feel its effects. There was no other explanation for the wild thoughts ricocheting around in his brain.

She was leaving, he realized. Rather than meander toward someone else, June appeared to be purposely aiming for the door.

He wanted to catch her.

Looking at the old Russian miner who'd been steadily talking to him for the past fifteen minutes, the current beau, he'd been informed, of June's grandmother, Kevin suddenly excused himself. He hadn't really heard half of what the man had been saying anyway, just nodding whenever there'd been a pause in the man's narrative. It didn't seem to faze the old man any.

"I'm sorry, there's someone I need to talk to."

"But of course, my boy. Go. Hurry. Now," Yuri all but ordered, sending him on his way.

Kevin made it to the front door just as June was about to go through it. His hand on her shoulder caught her attention. "You're leaving?"

She turned to look at him in surprise. She'd been

sure she'd seen the last of him this evening. As a matter of fact, she would have preferred it that way.

Her voice was crisp as she said, "I've got to get up early tomorrow, so I thought I should call it a night." She'd been the one who'd brought him here, so maybe an addendum was in order. She gave him one grudgingly. "I thought that April and Jimmy could take you home, seeing as how you're staying with them until the wedding anyway."

"Sure, no problem." He could feel the frost. Instinctively, he knew he deserved it. He nodded toward the parking area. "Walk you out?"

She didn't need anyone coming with her to her car. "I've been walking since—"

Taking matters into his own hands, he took her arm and guided her outside. "Don't you ever get tired of telling everyone how independent you are?"

As far as she was concerned, he was trespassing now, butting in where he had no business being. "No," she said stubbornly, "I don't. People have a habit of forgetting that I'm independent, because I'm still walking around with 'dew' all over me." Her eyebrows narrowed. "Wasn't that the way you put it?"

Yup, he was right. She was mad at him. He'd probably insulted her because he hadn't kissed her. But insulting her had been the furthest thing from his mind.

"Not quite." Kevin supposed apologies were in

order. "I didn't mean to get off on the wrong foot with you."

"You didn't get off on any foot at all."

If her glare was any colder, Kevin had a feeling he would have had to have been thawed out with a bonfire. "Then why do I have the impression that you're annoyed with me?"

She walked faster to her Jeep, refusing to look at him. "I'm not."

"One thing I was always good at," he told her tolerantly, "was spotting a lie."

Reaching her vehicle, she spun around to face him. "So now I'm not just a baby, I'm a liar, too?"

No one could ever accuse him of having a glib tongue. But at least it was an honest one. He threw himself on her mercy. "This isn't coming out right."

"Maybe it shouldn't come out at all." She yanked open the door to her vehicle. The sooner she got out of here, the better. She didn't know what had come over her before, all but throwing herself at Kevin. Maybe she just liked exercising her feminine wiles, she didn't know. All she knew was that she'd felt humiliated when he said he wasn't going to kiss her. "Good night, Kevin."

He caught her by the shoulders, turning her around to face him. "And maybe it should."

Captured between his hands, she was standing very close to him. So close that he could feel her breath as it entered and left her body. So close that he found his thoughts rebelling against the perfect order he'd filed them in. Anticipation telegraphed itself along the nerves that networked through him.

He continued to stumble through his apology, wishing for all the world that just once, he could have been granted Jimmy's smooth way with words. Jimmy was the operator in the family, not him. "If you're angry because I didn't kiss you—"

He'd pressed the wrong buttons. Or the right ones, depending on whose point of view was being observed. In any event, her blue eyes flashed at him: two tiny white-hot bolts of lightning aimed straight at his heart.

Furious, June yanked her shoulders free of his hold. "The hell I am. You think an awful lot of yourself, don't you, Quintano?"

"No," he told her quietly, his eyes never leaving hers, "I think a lot of you. A lot about you," he admitted softly without meaning to.

The next thing he knew, his hands were back on her shoulders, holding her in place. Gently.

A second after that, he lowered his head and brushed his lips against hers.

Softly, wistfully. Achingly gentle.

All of her life, she'd tried to be tough. To be one of the guys, except with curves, although she'd played down the latter, hiding them beneath jeans and overalls because, other than on her own terms and fleetingly, the last thing she wanted was to enter this male-female game that always came at such high stakes.

Sure, her brother and sister seemed happy now, far happier than she'd ever seen her own mother. And her grandmother was never happier than when she was involved with a man.

But that wasn't her way.

She wasn't going to get tangled up in anything that had the capability of stripping her soul down to the last layer, of mortally wounding her so that she couldn't recover, the way her mother hadn't recovered after her father had left them.

The others thought she was too young to remember. But she remembered. Vividly remembered. The image of her mother, pale and wan, sitting by the window and staring vacant-eyed out at the lonely terrain, waiting for a man who never returned, waiting until the day she died, was firmly imprinted on her brain.

And it wasn't going to happen to her.

Ever.

When she kissed a man, she kissed him on her own terms and then went on, free-spirited and unaffected. That had always been the case, without exception.

Except, that wasn't happening now.

This wasn't on her own terms and she wasn't moving on at the moment of contact, wasn't being disinterested or bored.

What she was being, was melted.

The very gentleness of the kiss was causing a huge core meltdown within her. So much so that she had to wrap her arms around Kevin's neck and hold on for all she was worth before there was nothing left of her but a warm puddle pooling at his feet.

And when the kiss deepened, as neither of them had planned it would, it ensnared both of them even as they struggled to break free.

The woman tasted of desire and all that was forbidden, all that he'd denied himself these long years. All that he'd missed.

Without meaning to, he kissed her harder, longer, and felt himself falling down a winding abyss filled with every northern light that had ever been conceived.

And the path back to firm ground had disintegrated.

Chapter Five

"He is kissing her!"

Excited, Yuri waved Ursula over to the window just as she'd completed her rounds, bidding Max and April goodbye.

"Come, Ursula, you are missing it." He waved to Ursula again.

Enthused, Ursula elbowed her way through the crowd, moving far more swiftly and gracefully than women half her age. Her eyes were eager as she joined her current beau.

From his vantage point, Yuri had a clear view of the parking lot where June had left her vehicle. And where the young woman and Kevin were now standing, oblivious to the rest of the world.

The trim salt-and-pepper beard on Yuri's cheeks spread widely as he pointed to the couple outside.

Ursula wiggled into the space right before him, then sighed.

"About time." She nodded her approval. "Handsome devil." Looking over her shoulder, Ursula slanted a glance at the man behind her. "Not as handsome as you, of course."

"Of course," he echoed, humor curving his generous mouth.

"But there's a lot of potential there." She turned away as the couple drew apart. "Hope they've both got the good sense to know that."

"And if they do not?" He knew the answer to that. Hades's postmistress was well-known for arranging people's lives when things were moving too slowly for her liking. It only proved she cared.

One shoulder lifted in a half shrug. She knew what he was thinking.

"Nothing wrong in prodding a slow couple on their way." She thought of her best triumph. "Like I did for April with my heart trouble."

Yuri gave the love of his life a knowing look and chucked her under the chin fondly. "There are some things, Ninotchka, that even you cannot control. Although, those things are not many, I must agree."

The indignation that might have been generated never materialized. Instead, her eyes crinkled into a pleased smile. "You do know how to turn a lady's head."

He laughed at the thought. "I do not want to turn your head. I want it just where it is." He ran his forefinger over the outline of her mouth. "Within range of my lips. Home?"

"Home." And then she looked out the window. "But let's give them a couple of minutes."

As always, he agreed. Yuri knew when he had a good thing going.

He had to come up for air.

The thought beat against Kevin's brain even as reluctance to part from her flooded his veins. Air was not nearly as sweet, as heady, as kissing June's lips.

But if he didn't get some soon, he was in danger of having his knees buckle out from under him, and that would be an embarrassment he wasn't sure he could live down. He had a feeling Hades wasn't a place that let things die quietly. Movie theater or not, entertainment was in scarce supply here.

Steady, June, steady. She drew her head back as she felt him do the same. If she didn't know better, she would have said they were having another earthquake. The ground felt as if it was shimmying beneath her feet.

But he wasn't moving, so the earthquake had to be an internal one.

Hers.

She was careful to draw air back into her lungs slowly. "So, that's what you think of me," she murmured. Desperate not to look like some thunderstruck teenager, she'd leaped on the last thing he'd said to her before the flares had gone off in her head.

Before he'd kissed her and redefined the boundaries of the known universe.

June knew that she was young and not all that experienced, but she didn't need to have led her grandmother's flamboyant life to know that what had just happened here was something special. If there'd been snow on the ground, she had a feeling it would have melted in a circle around her feet.

Still feeling wobbly, she reached for the car door and held on to it, hoping she wasn't being obvious. Forcing a smile to her lips, she cleared her throat.

"I'd better be getting back to my place. Jimmy'll take you home."

Was she making any sense? she wondered. Her thoughts were assaulting her like pillaging Vikings, coming in from all sides without any uniformity at all.

Why did she feel so wonderful and sad at the same time? Why did she feel like laughing and crying, and staying and fleeing?

What the hell *was* that?

Kevin took a step back away from her, wanting only to step forward.

Wanting to kiss her again. And again.

He was just lonely, he insisted silently. And she was a beautiful woman, even if she did nothing to bring that out.

He realized that he was supposed to say something here. His mind scrambled for words.

"Right." He pointed behind him needlessly. "I'll just go back inside and find him." *Provided I can still walk.*

June nodded, then got into her Jeep, suddenly collapsing in her seat as if all the air had just been let out of her. She took a deep breath before starting the vehicle, hoping he wasn't watching. Hoping no one had been watching. If they had, this was going to wreak havoc with her image. Hard to pretend that she could care less about men and romance when she'd just been hermetically sealed to one.

And wishing she still was.

As if to deny the existence of the thought, June stomped down on the accelerator and roared off into the night.

Kevin sat at the sturdy wooden table, nursing a mug of coffee.

Suddenly, his brother Jimmy stumbled into the kitchen. "What are you doing up?"

"Can't sleep," Kevin muttered, and glanced in his direction.

Which was true. He couldn't. He'd tried to tell himself that it was jet lag, but travel time from Seattle to

Anchorage hadn't been that long and besides, he'd remained in the same time zone, so that wasn't the culprit for his inability to fall asleep. And neither was the strange habits of the sun, which seemed to barely disappear in the sky before it put in another appearance.

He knew why he couldn't sleep, but he wasn't about to put it into words. Formless and unidentified, it might stand a chance of going away.

Kevin nodded toward the coffeemaker sitting on the granite counter. "I made some coffee. Hope you don't mind."

Already at the counter, Jimmy laughed as he poured himself a cup. He brought himself over to the table and sank down on the chair opposite his brother. Felt like old times, he thought, taking a long sip of the thick, black liquid. A distant smile curved his mouth. "I remember your coffee. Thick enough to grease the axles of that first taxi you had."

Kevin thought of the old car. Squat, wide and yellow, there'd been almost a hundred thousand miles on it when he'd inherited it after buying the business from his old boss.

"Damn thing kept breaking down. Almost spent more time trying to fix it than driving it." He laughed fondly. His feelings hadn't been quite so fond at the time. Kevin shook his head as he took another sip. "Seems like a million years ago."

Jimmy wrapped his hands around his mug. He

looked up at his brother, studying Kevin's face. "Why did you sell the business?"

Kevin frowned, shrugging as he looked away. "Seemed like—"

"Don't give me the same garbage you gave Lily." Jimmy wanted to know the real reason, not the one his brother was handing out. "You loved that business."

"No," Kevin corrected adamantly. "I loved all of *you*. The taxi service just helped me keep us together, that's all. Now that we're all apart..." His voice drifted off. There didn't seem to be anything to say as he shrugged his shoulders.

Jimmy didn't have to fill in the blanks. He knew how Kevin felt about them. His older brother had sacrificed having a life of his own so that all of them could pursue their dreams. He'd always felt guilty about that.

Impulse had him leaning in to his brother. "Then move up here," Jimmy urged. "I mean, it's not like you've exactly got a life back in Seattle." He stopped suddenly, realizing that maybe he was assuming too much. Maybe Kevin had moved on with his life now that the rest of them were all here. "You don't, do you? I mean, there's been no femme fatale to snare you since I left, right? Lily would have said something—" He thought of his older sister as a little bit of a control freak, trying to run everyone's life while neglecting to put her own in order—until Max had come along.

Kevin laughed softly to himself at his brother's choice of words. "No, there's no femme fatale, but it's not that easy."

Jimmy believed in seizing opportunities when they came. Falling for April had taught him that. "It's only as complicated as you make it."

There was a delayed echo in his head. "Funny, June said the same thing."

"Did she now?" His voice sounded a wee bit too innocent to be convincing, Jimmy thought, annoyed with himself. He tried hard to keep a straight face, but it wasn't easy. Ursula had already told the family about what she'd seen last night. Jimmy pretended to be taken with the contents of his mug. "Pretty girl, that June."

"Hadn't noticed," Kevin said.

Frowning, Jimmy set down his cup. Taking his wrist, his brother placed his fingers over his pulse. Kevin pulled his hand away and looked at him. "What are you doing?"

"Checking to see just when you died," Jimmy responded frankly.

Kevin sighed. "All right, I noticed. I noticed she was very pretty," he amended. "I also noticed that she's barely out of her teens."

"Three years is hardly 'barely,' Kev. Mom was nineteen when she married Dad."

"And Dad was twenty-two. I'm not." A tiny bit of exasperation entered Kevin's voice. "So what's your point?"

Jimmy drained his cup, now fully fortified to do battle with the best of them. "My point is that you've spent the last umpteen years of your life working your tail off for us and you never got to be twenty-two—or nineteen for that matter. My way of thinking, since June grew up faster than the average girl, that puts you at about the same age."

Kevin laughed shortly. "Only if you flunked math." And then he replayed the last thing Jimmy said. "What do you mean, she grew up faster?"

Jimmy reviewed the highlights. "Abandoned by her father, watching her mother sink into an irreversible depression." He rose and crossed to the coffeemaker. Maybe one more cup wouldn't hurt. "Leaves one hell of an impression on a kid." The smile that played on his lips was enigmatic. "Makes you look at things differently than the average person." Knowing how resistant Kevin was to the suggestion of romance, he tried a different approach. "Kev, while you're here, relax, enjoy yourself. Open up your mind to things."

"I've never been closed minded."

Only when it came to his own life, Jimmy thought. He searched for a tactful way to say that. "No, you've actually been too busy all this time to think about things other than providing for us and meeting the bills. Extraneous thoughts weren't welcomed." Crossing back to the table, he put his mug down and looked at Kevin. "Welcome them now."

"Since when have you hung up a psychiatrist's shingle? I thought your specialty was the heart." Kevin didn't like attention being focused on him. Liked other people, even people he loved, trying to "fix" his life when it wasn't broken even less.

Jimmy's eyes met his and he grinned. "It is my specialty."

"Good morning."

Both men turned toward the doorway at the sound of the sleepy female voice. April stumbled over to the counter.

"Is that coffee I smell?"

"Help yourself," Kevin invited, then looked at Jimmy and lowered his voice. "Not another word," he cautioned, then added weight to the warning. "I can still probably take you."

Jimmy laughed. Working had not made his brother flabby. Kevin looked as likely to bench-press a cab as to drive one. "Probably."

Kevin brought the Jeep to a stop before the farmhouse and got out. For a moment, he stood in front of the building, studying it. Dark and dreary, some of the wood desperately needed replacing. And it cried out for a fresh coat of paint. The last had probably been applied more than two decades ago.

The place, he thought, needed a hell of a lot of work. It looked every moment of its age, having suffered the hard winters here, and come out looking the worse for it.

What made June want to stay here when, according to Jimmy, she had a small place in town?

He'd come here by himself, using Jimmy's Jeep after dropping his brother off at the clinic. It was Jimmy's turn to open early. April had offered to drive him over here later, but he'd turned her down. Kevin liked exploring on his own.

Armed with a map, there wasn't any place he couldn't find. Finding the farm that June's parents had once shared with their children had been relatively easy.

It looked like a place where dreams had been born and died, he thought, studying the exterior. He wondered if she planned on at least painting it before another winter came to assault the old building.

Stepping onto the front porch, he heard it creak in protest as he crossed to the front door. He knocked once, but there was no answer. Knocking again a bit more forcefully, he found that the door wobbled in its jamb and that, when he turned the knob, it opened.

The fact that the door, and thus the house, was unlocked offended his sense of security. He didn't believe in leaving doors unlocked or in taking needless chances.

Someone had to talk to the woman to make her see

that she was leaving herself open to any psychopath, not to mention the occasional wandering grizzly. Lily had been vividly descriptive about being treed by a bear her first week in Hades. Max had been there to save her. There might not be anyone to save June in a similar situation.

He didn't want to just walk in and surprise June. There was no telling what she might be doing. But she wasn't answering his knock and he had come out to see her for a reason.

Making a decision, he cautiously opened the door and stepped just inside.

"June?" There was no answer. He raised his voice. "June, it's Kevin. Jimmy's brother," he added as an addendum, telling himself that it sounded lame even as he said it. He might as well have referred to himself as the guy who played tonsil hockey with her last night.

She didn't seem to be inside the house. At least, not where she could hear him. He went from room to room within the small house. The woman, he quickly realized, was never going to get a job as a housekeeper. There was clothing scattered throughout the house, mixed in with newspapers, books on farming, and various foodstuffs that obviously had never made it to the cupboards.

He wondered what kind of a kitchen she kept. Probably the kind to make Lily shriek.

"June?" he called again.

Music came from the rear of the house. He made his way to what he discovered was the kitchen. She'd left a radio on, but there was no sign of June.

Curious and more than a little concerned, Kevin opened the back screen door and walked outside. The large yard eventually led to the barn. The barn doors were open and, as he drew closer, the odor of livestock assaulted him full force.

Coughing, he entered and waited until his eyes adjusted to the dimness. The stalls, he noted, were empty. Whatever animals were housed here, he reasoned, were probably out in the field, feeding.

But where was she?

A loud curse, turning the air blue, answered his silent question. It came from behind the barn.

Rounding the building, he found June sitting on the ground, nursing her thumb, which she'd popped into her mouth. A myriad of tools were haphazardly spread out around her. It looked as if a hardware store had exploded. A tractor that had known better times was behind her.

He crouched down beside her, ready to examine the injury. "Are you all right?"

Self-conscious, she drew her hand out of reach. "I will be when I get the use of my thumb back." Rising to her feet, she examined the mashed digit, then raised her eyes to his face. "Come for an encore?"

Amusement played on her lips. For her part, she'd decided to view what had happened last night lightly.

Because to do anything else was far too scary for her to contemplate.

"Come to apologize, actually."

"Why?" She looked at him more closely. Had he come by to say that he was sorry he had kissed her? The thought stung and she had no idea why. June turned away from him and pretended to focus her attention back to the errant tractor. She purposely kept her voice nonchalant. "I thought it was rather nice, as far as kisses went."

"It was. Very nice." No, *nice* wasn't a word he would have used here. It was far too bland to describe what he'd felt. "Better than nice—"

June looked at him. "Then why are you apologizing?"

"Because you're you and I'm me."

If there was something that made less sense, she wasn't aware of it. She cocked her head, as if trying to delve into his head. "Did those X-ray machines at the airports do something to your brain? That didn't make any sense."

He supposed she was right. He wasn't even sure what he was really doing here. "I'm not making too much sense this morning." When she looked at him quizzically, he gave her the first excuse he could think of. "I didn't sleep a lot last night."

She picked up a torque wrench and turned back to the tractor again. "Most tourists have trouble adjusting to the fact that the sun sets about ten and rises about three in August.''

''That wasn't the problem.'' He stood looking over her shoulder, trying not to notice how slender it was. ''I've never had any trouble sleeping before.''

Annoyed with the machine she was trying to resurrect, she looked at him over her shoulder. ''So what's giving you trouble now?''

He decided to be candid, and honest. ''My conscience.''

Her smile was wry. ''Should have left that at the airport, too.''

''June, I—''

She stopped what she figured was another apology in its tracks. Why did men always think they were the ones who made things happen, who took the initiative?

June swung around, her hands on her hips, the torque wrench dangling from her fingertips. ''Nothing happens to me that I don't want to happen. Let's just leave it at that, okay? Now, if you don't mind, I've got a tractor to bring back from the dead.''

He gravitated to the neutral terrain. ''What's wrong with it?''

''I just told you, it's dead.'' She waved the wrench at it. ''No matter what I do to it, the engine just won't turn over.''

Though he'd kept a regular mechanic at the cab

company, he was a fair mechanic on his own. "Mind if I take a look at it?"

Her temper, she found, was rather short today. "It doesn't need to be looked at, it needs to be fixed."

"Can't do that if I don't look at it first."

"I've looked at it. I've *been* looking at it for the last day and a half." In disgust, she threw down the torque wrench and stepped away, knowing that if she kept at it any longer in her present state of mind, she might just use the wrench to take apart the rest of it and chuck it all. "Be my guest."

"Thanks, don't mind if I do." Kevin rolled up his sleeves.

For the first time since he'd arrived in Hades, he felt useful. And at home.

Chapter Six

"Try it."

Just coming out of the house with a glass of iced coffee for Kevin—all that she could manage to scrounge up on short notice in the way of a sociable beverage—June stopped dead in her tracks.

Not because of his short instruction, given as he waved at the tractor, but because in the time that it had taken her to go inside and try to locate something other than the two bottles of beer in her refrigerator to offer him, Kevin had finally surrendered to the heat and stripped off his damp shirt.

She'd already noticed, albeit somewhat unwillingly, how the material had clung to his body. But the difference between her speculation and reality was the difference between a Monet and a six-year-old's crayon rendition of a lake. The man's torso looked as if Michelangelo had studied it before creating his statue of David.

Kevin's chest was sculpted, tanned and gleaming. She pressed her lips together to make sure her mouth wasn't hanging open.

How did a man who, until very recently, ran a cab company and spent most of his time in enclosures of one sort or another come off looking like a model in search of a product to push? In Kevin's present state, he could have sold argyle socks to Australian Aborigine tribesmen in the wild.

Kevin looked in her direction, a quizzical expression on his face and she realized that she'd all but solidified in place. Allowing the sizzling effect of his appearance to penetrate further, she thawed out immediately.

Clearing her throat as she rejoined the animated world, June looked at the tractor skeptically, trying very hard to focus her thoughts on the piece of machinery and not the man holding the wrench.

It wasn't easy.

Tractor, think tractor. She stared at the antiquated machine that had been housed in the barn for the better part of a decade and a half. Overhauling it, she'd gotten it to work several times, but never for long and on this last effort, it had completely given up the ghost no matter what she tried.

June chewed on her lower lip. He'd been working on the tractor for the better part of three hours. Granted, he seemed to have gotten all the pieces back to where they belonged or, at least, off the ground, but that was no proof that he'd done any better a job than she had in all of her previous recent attempts to get the engine to run again.

She took a few steps forward. "What did you do?" she wanted to know.

Since she was holding the glass out, Kevin assumed the iced coffee was intended for him. He took the glass from her.

"Just try it," he urged again, then took a long, long sip, grateful for the cold liquid. He rubbed the glass along his brow. Sweat poured off him. "If it works, then I'll explain what I did. Otherwise, there's no point."

Move, think, talk, she instructed herself sternly when she realized she'd suddenly become glued into place again. *Do anything but stare at him. He's just a man. Lots of H_2O, skin, hair, fat cells, that's all.*

But somehow, whoever had created Kevin Quintano had found a magical combination that took mere flesh and fashioned it into something temptingly delectable.

Shivers threatened to run up and down her spine, embarrassing her.

June looked away. She had to get a grip on herself and these strange thoughts that insisted on leaping around in her head. Who cared what he looked like? Could he fix her tractor? should have been the only thing on her mind.

Taking her keys out of her hip pocket, June got up on the tractor, frowned dubiously at the machine and inserted the key in the ignition. She turned it and, after a sputter, the engine coughed into life, where it remained until she turned it off.

"I did that the last time," she told Kevin loftily, determined not to be impressed. "It didn't turn over again."

Kevin indicated the ignition. "Go ahead and try it again, then."

Try it again. She was getting to hate that phrase. She didn't know why, but it made her feel inept. Especially when she turned the key and the engine turned over again, this time without emitting either a sputter or a cough.

June sat in the tractor seat, letting the machine vibrate beneath her, a stallion wanting nothing more than to be set free.

Was Kevin like that?

Her eyes widened as her silent question sank in. God, where had that come from?

She wondered if she could be suffering from some sort of heat stroke. That had to be it. It was an inordinately hot day for the region. But she'd spent less time out in the sun than he had.

A mosquito buzzed around her neck and she slapped it away, relieved for the simple diversion.

"All right," she said, getting off. "*Now* will you tell me what you did to it?" She fixed him with an almost exasperated look. "Or is this just a matter of the laying on of hands and healing the damn thing?"

She sounded awfully impatient for a woman who'd just had an important piece of machinery repaired. "No healing, no laying." He laughed, pleased with his own effort.

Prolonging the moment, Kevin set the drained glass down against the back of the barn. He wasn't ordinarily given to drama of any kind; that was exclusively Lily's department. But the moment seemed to beg for it. Especially in view of June's temperamental behavior. She needed to learn to mellow out a little.

"But you're going to keep it a secret." She frowned at him. This was so typical of a male.

He looked at her innocently, wondering what kind of people she was accustomed to dealing with. Had they treated her like an anomaly of nature because of her skills, or like a younger sibling who always insisted on doing what they did?

"Why would I do that?"

She blew out a breath, knowing she was being short-tempered. But given the situation, as well as the weather, it was hard not to. She thought of the walls she'd run up against.

"I don't know, men are very territorial when it comes to sharing what they know, thinking that the puny female mind isn't capable of absorbing those kinds of technical details."

He studied June for a moment before answering. Temper made her features sharper. Also more vivid. "I never thought of your mind as puny, or particularly female for that matter."

"I don't know whether to take offense or be flattered."

He made it easy for her. "No offense intended," he told her.

Then, before she could say anything else, he launched into a detailed explanation of what he'd attempted to do and had obviously succeeded in accomplishing. He noted that, as she listened, a grudging admiration entered June's eyes.

"No big mystery, really," he concluded. "Sometimes the simplest details are the ones that are overlooked."

Turning from her, he reached for the shirt he'd left slung over a nail on the fence that served as a make-shift corral. He'd been told that once this had been a horse ranch. He was about to put the shirt on again when June stopped him, all but grabbing it out of his hands.

"Wait, don't."

He didn't understand what had made her spring into action like that. Looking around him didn't make things any clearer. "What?"

She realized she'd put a little too much emotion into the entreaty. But that was because she hadn't wanted to see him slip the shirt on just yet.

"I mean, it's damp." She turned it into a challenge. "You don't want to put on a damp, sweaty shirt, do you, Kevin?"

"Don't see as I have much choice." His eyes swept over her. "I don't think anything you might have would fit me."

Why did she suddenly feel as if her throat was closing up, making it hard for her to swallow. Or breathe? "I can hang it up."

He could just hear Jimmy if he came back to the house shirtless. He spread his arms out wide. "What do I do in the meantime?"

Stay just like that. This was getting out of hand. June censored herself. "I've got more work you can do while it's drying—if you're game."

He had the time and he liked to work, so that wasn't a problem. But he was curious. He looked around, as if to confirm his impression. "No other hired hands?"

Was that a judgmental tone she heard in his voice? Her own became defensive. "Not at the moment."

He knew that as far as farms went, this wasn't exactly huge, but it wasn't tiny, either. And a lot of work went into running a farm. She had both a crop and several head of cattle. "Isn't this rather a large undertaking for just one woman?"

Her eyes flashed as she raised her chin. "It's not exactly like I'm hitching myself up to a plow and pulling it along the furrows." Sarcasm dripped from her voice. "At least, not now that you've brought my tractor back from the dead."

He got the feeling that she was waiting for him to rub her nose in it. He shrugged casually.

"You would have figured it out on your own if I hadn't come along," he assured her. Then, to her surprise, he placed his fingers on her chin and pushed it down slightly. "No need to get on your high horse, June. You take offense far too fast, especially when none's intended." Her attitude didn't make sense to him. "I thought men would treat women like princesses here."

"They do." She let out a short, exasperated breath, but this time, it wasn't directed toward him. "But princesses aren't equals."

He couldn't argue with her there. "No, they're usually superior."

A slight smile curved her mouth. "The men around here don't think that far ahead."

"You mean like that Haggerty?" He supposed that was a slip. He shouldn't have mentioned the man, but the way the miner had looked at June, as if he'd liked to own her, had lingered on his mind.

"Him," she acknowledged. "Some of the others."
She didn't want to talk about the local talent, or lack
thereof. "Are you game?" June took his shirt from
the nail. "You can work just as long as it takes to
dry your shirt." She held it out before her, pretending
to make a judgment while she was really taking the
opportunity to look more closely at him again. God,
but he was rock solid. "Shouldn't take long in this
heat."

He looked around, seeing plenty of places he could
get started. The steps on her porch looked as if they
were about to crack apart in several places. A person
could sustain a nasty twist of an ankle stepping down
at the wrong time.

"What have you got in mind?"

She thought of the fence she'd been working on in
between cursing at the tractor. "I've got some rotting
fence posts that need replacing." She'd left the new
posts beside the ones that needed to be pulled out,
intending on getting to that next. "Are you good with
your hands?" She glanced at them.

He couldn't help the response that came to his lips
as they curved. "Never had any complaints."

No, she'd wager that he hadn't. What she didn't
quite get was why he was still alone, especially now
that he didn't have a family making all those demands
on him.

Not her business, she told herself tersely.

"All right then, follow me." She waved him over

to her car, an all-terrain vehicle she'd lovingly restored while she still owned the auto repair shop.

He took the shovel and the sledgehammer from her as she went to pick up each. "By the way," he said as he followed her to the vehicle, "do you know you left the radio on in the kitchen?"

"I know." She waited until he deposited the tools in the rear of the car. "It keeps me company when I walk into the house." She'd almost said that it kept her from being lonely, which was something she didn't want to admit to him, or to anyone for that matter. June started the car, then, because she could almost feel the effects of his expression, she glanced at him. "What are you smiling about?"

"Nothing, I was just surprised at how much we have in common."

"Because we both can fix engines?" She thought that was already a given. Why would he be smiling about that now?

He thought of the house on Maple Street, the one that seemed so empty now. "No, because we both make sure there's some kind of noise in the house to keep from getting lonely."

She shot him a look. "I didn't say I get lonely. I just like music." And then she took the edge off her voice. Some of her defensiveness abated in the face of his admission. He'd surprised her. Men didn't usually admit to things like this. "You get lonely?"

He saw no shame in it. "Yes."

All things considered, that didn't make much sense to her. She could see getting lonely here. The winter nights were mournfully long and even now, in the summer, the isolation at times seemed all-pervading.

"But you live in a big city." He could go out his door at any time and find a host of people. She had to get into her car and drive for miles before she could see another face.

"Easy to feel lonely in a crowd," he told her. He thought of her last night at the Salty. The saloon had been filled with wall-to-wall people, all of whom she knew by name. Being lonely in a crowd wasn't something she was familiar with. "Besides, it's the sound of the others I miss. Jimmy and Alison lived in the house until they came up here, and even Lily was in and out so much, there were times I forgot she had her own place." He looked out at the wide terrain. "Having them all gone makes it very quiet."

For a moment, she felt as if they were sharing something very intimate, as intimate as the kiss had been, except with far less kick to it. "And you don't like that?"

Kevin shook his head. "No, not much." Not at all, really, he added silently.

She slanted a long glance at him. "Huh, imagine that." They were close in her family, although they never talked about it. She doubted if she'd ever hear Max admit something like this to her. Max loved having his own space, so much so that at times she wondered how Lily was going to fit into it. "You're a very unusual man, you know that?" she said softly. She settled back in her seat as she drove. "I can remember my father always telling us to be quiet."

Parents were always telling their children to be quiet. As far as he was concerned, quiet was highly overrated. "What else do you remember about your father?"

She stared off in front of her. "His not being there," she said tersely.

Kevin always knew when to leave something alone. And he did.

Stretching, Kevin leaned his arms on top of the sledgehammer he'd been wielding. Each of his arms felt as if they weighed thirty pounds apiece. He watched as the vehicle approached him.

Finally, he thought.

He wrapped his hand around the shank of the sledgehammer, depositing it into the back seat. "I was wondering when you'd get around to coming back for me." Turning, he picked up the shovel and threw it in next to the other tool.

Time had gotten away from her. June looked at the posts, then at him in surprise. He was faster than he appeared. "You're all done."

He shrugged, wiping the sweat from his brow with the back of his wrist. "There were only four posts."

It was an effort for her to tear her eyes away. His

muscles were rippling. And her stomach was tightening. "I thought it would take you longer. Your shirt's dry." She held it up.

Yes, but he wasn't. Kevin took it from her, debating putting it on. Climbing into the vehicle, he decided to leave the shirt on his lap.

Having him so close to her, sweaty, gleaming and naked from the waist up, had an unsettling effect on her rebelling stomach. Her hands tightened on the wheel. "Why aren't you putting your shirt on?"

He looked slightly amused. "Because, while my throat's dry, I'm not. If I put it on now, it'll just get damp again."

Was he laughing at her? Was there color creeping into her cheeks? She had to stop herself from raising her chin defiantly. "Sorry, I forgot to leave you some water. I'll get you back to the house as fast as possible."

"That would be nice." His lips felt parched. So did the rest of him. "So would lunch." He looked up at the sun as she drove back to the farmhouse. "Or is it past that time? I didn't wear a watch today and I can't really tell up here."

"It's closer to dinner." More guilt. She should have fed him, but then, she really wasn't used to having company. Her socializing was done either at the Salty or at the house of one of her relatives. She was never the one who did the entertaining. She bit her lip as she slanted a glance at him. "You must be starving."

"I could eat." His stomach rumbled. Kevin grinned. "Possibly a small horse."

"I don't have one of those." She thought of the contents of her refrigerator. "But I do have a steak. You're welcome to it."

He got the impression that there was nothing else. "What are you going to have?"

She shrugged. "I'll find something. Cereal. Toast. A piece of fruit."

All things a bachelor might eat in a pinch. His grin widened. "I take it you're not very domestic."

June frowned. Her grandmother had always gotten on her case about that. She told him exactly what she told her, except a little more coolly. "I fixed cars, not meals."

"There's that defensiveness again." He was beginning to think that was simply her way. "I'm just asking questions, June, trying to get a handle on things."

"Why?" She looked at him. "Where are you planning on carrying it?"

He saw the farmhouse in the distance. "Have you always been this suspicious of people?"

"Not people, strangers."

He didn't like the way she slapped the label on him. "I'd think that after sweating over your tractor and your rotting fence poles, I wouldn't be that much of a stranger to you."

"A stranger is someone I haven't known since birth." June backtracked a little.

"That means I'm always going to be a stranger to you."

June shrugged self-consciously. "I guess we can work on that."

"Sounds like a plan to me."

"Yeah, maybe." Arriving at the house, she pulled up the hand brake. The next minute, he was getting out and striding up the front steps as if he owned the house, instead of her.

Jumping out on her side, she was quick to follow him inside. He headed straight for the kitchen.

"What do you think you're doing?" she asked as he opened the refrigerator.

Kevin took out the steak, a half-empty bottle of tomato sauce, a wilting onion and what appeared to be a half-filled container of rice. He deposited them on the narrow counter. "Well, you said you weren't domestic—"

She moved so that she was between him and the counter. "So?"

Kevin put his hands on her shoulders and very patiently moved her out of the way. "So who do you think taught Lily the basic fundamentals?"

"You?"

He laughed as he looked for a pot. There was one dented Dutch oven in the cabinet beneath the sink.

He took out his prize. "Don't look so surprised, some of the world's best chefs are men."

She crossed her arms before her. "You fix cars and cook."

"Among other things." Reaching for the salt on the counter, he stopped and looked at her. "Unless, of course, you feel I'm trespassing."

That would be cutting off her nose to spite her face. Besides, she was hungry, and curious to boot. She stepped back, waving him on. "Hey, trespass away. I never liked to cook, it was just something I had to do."

"Good?" Dinner was on the table and he'd been watching her eat now for two minutes without any comment. Although he was never one who fished for compliments, his curiosity got the best of him.

Very slowly, she drew the fork from her lips and swallowed. Part of her had been hoping he'd fail, but he hadn't. Reluctantly she nodded. "Good."

It was hard not to miss her tone. "You say that grudgingly."

She lifted one shoulder in a careless gesture. "I was just wondering if there was something you weren't good at."

He laughed shortly and mostly at himself. "Lots of things." He said the first thing that came to mind. "Conversations, for instance."

"You seem to be holding your own."

"You're not being demanding."

Putting down her fork, she looked at him. "And if I were?"

He thought of some of the dates he'd allowed himself to be set up with. "Then I'd probably shut up and be quiet."

"Talk," she urged, digging in again. "I like the sound of your voice."

Her head down, she missed the smile that rose to his lips as he looked at her. No one had ever said that to him before.

Chapter Seven

Turning from the sink, June carefully wiped her hands on a dish towel that seldom saw any use.

Ordinarily she'd let dishes sit in the sink and get to them whenever she needed a clean plate. Drying more than one dish at any given time was unheard of. But when dinner was over, she'd been quick to start washing the dishes she and Kevin had used. She didn't want him thinking she was completely hopeless on the domestic front.

Why that should matter was something she felt was better left unexplored for the time being.

She looked at him as she set the towel on the counter. He was just finishing up the glasses they'd used. "You're frowning."

It wasn't actually a frown but more what Alison had once referred to as his "thoughtful face." He let the protest ride.

"Just trying to figure out what time it is." He'd forgotten his watch this morning. Kevin shook his head as he glanced toward the wide window over the sink. "I haven't a clue."

He shrugged philosophically. Time really didn't matter right now, he supposed. For the first time in his life, he didn't need to be anywhere at any particular given time. It felt rather odd not to have a constricting schedule, as if he was suddenly leading someone else's life. Someone who wasn't productive.

He was still trying to figure out if he liked living that kind of life or not.

Kevin looked out the kitchen window again. The sky was as blue as it had been this morning. The sun seemed to have been superglued into place, offering him no clues as to the hour.

He retired the glass he was drying to the counter. "You get the impression that time is standing still up here."

"Sometimes it does."

June put the glass into the cupboard beside its mate. She owned exactly four glasses, enough for herself, her siblings and her grandmother. The family was growing. Maybe it was time to get more.

She closed the cupboard and turned to face Kevin.

"They like to say that we march to a different drummer in Alaska. That time spent here is richer."

That had a nice ring to it. He studied her for a moment and couldn't decide if she was putting him on or not. "How do you feel about that?"

She didn't even have to think before she spoke. "Well, I know that I wouldn't want to be anywhere else in the world." She was standing too close to him, she realized. And something vibrated inside her. "But you should probably be getting back."

That had come out of left field. "Have I overstayed my welcome?"

She pressed her lips together. That had sounded a little abrupt, as if she was trying to get rid of him. She probably needed a little help in her people skills, she supposed. "No, but if you don't turn up soon, April might send Max looking for you. It's about six o'clock." She took the wet dish towel from his hand and carefully spread it out on the rack to dry. Try as she might, she couldn't talk him out of doing the dishes with her. The whole thing had seemed oddly intimate and she felt strangely out of focus tonight. "You've been here for a good part of the day."

Emphasis on "good," Kevin thought. Besides, April wouldn't be the one looking for him. He'd promised to spend the night at Alison's.

"Have I? It feels as if I just got here." Which was almost the truth. Even though he hadn't been aware of the passing of the hours, they still had somehow managed to whiz by. He smiled at her. "Like I said, time seems to stand still up here."

She looked up at him and for a second, she thought he was going to kiss her. Or maybe that was just her own wishful thinking. June looked away, glancing at his wrist. "Maybe you need to wear your watch."

"Maybe."

What he knew was that he needed to leave before it became awkward. Before he found another excuse to stay. Because he wanted one. Wanted an excuse to remain just where he was, talking to her, looking at her.

He knew what this was. Loneliness, plain and simple, fueled by the sight of what had always been missing from his life. A fresh-faced, beautiful young woman. This was nothing more than his last attempt at snaring a bit of youth and drawing it into his life.

He knew he should know better.

He *did* know better, and yet, here he stood, wishing for a reason to remain. Wanting to take her into his arms and hold her.

And kiss her.

"I'd better go," he agreed, and began to walk to the front door.

She fell into step beside him.

The soft music from her radio followed them to the front door, wrapping itself tightly around them with each note. Creating an intimacy that was hard to shake.

Where were the fast dance numbers when you needed them? June wondered.

When he stopped at the door and looked down at her, she felt her breath catch in her throat. Was he going to kiss her?

Oh God, she hoped so.

Stop it, you can't think like that. What's wrong with you?

Suddenly tongue-tied, she looked for something besides a love ballad to fill the air. "Well, thanks for your help."

He glanced around. The entranceway was dark, like the rest of the house. It seemed that the sunlight couldn't manage to push its way inside despite the windows. "I've hardly made a dent."

She didn't understand. He'd done everything she'd asked. More. "What do you mean? The tractor's running fine and, because of you, I don't have to struggle with the fence posts anymore."

He gestured around the room. Trim needed replacing, walls needed painting, and she could definitely stand to have new windows and doors put in. "Seems to me that this old house could use a bit of work."

June opened her mouth instantly. Her first inclination was to deny his assumption, but she was afraid that her nose would grow. If ever a place needed work, it was this one.

So instead, she merely shrugged and rocked on the balls of her feet. "I'll get to it by and by."

Kevin stuck his hands into his back pockets, wanting to look anywhere but at her face. He couldn't look anywhere *but* her face.

His thoughts took off, multiplying. "Listen, I'm going to be here until the wedding. I told Lily I wanted to help her with the arrangements. She didn't say anything, but I've got the definite feeling that my butting in would be about as welcome as blotches on a supermodel. I hate just hanging around, doing nothing—"

She knew where this was going and wasn't all that sure it was a good idea. "You could play tourist."

But he shook his head. "I don't play very well." It wasn't that he didn't think the terrain was beautiful, but he wasn't the type to take in scenery from dawn to dusk, especially since right now, the time in between lasted forever. "What I'm best at is work. I felt good today for the first time since I sold the business. Since *before* I sold the business," he corrected himself." He took his hands out of his pockets and held them up for her benefit. "Two hands, no waiting. What do you say I put them to work for you? For the house," Kevin amended in case she thought he meant something a little more handy than he'd actually intended.

"I can't pay you—" she began. And she wasn't into charity, she was going to add, but she never got the opportunity.

"Did I ask for money?" he wanted to know.

She wished he'd stop interrupting her. "No, but—"

He didn't want to be shot down and the only viable way, apparently, to keep flying was to outtalk her. "Actually, I should be paying you—for allowing me to keep my sanity."

The wind left her sails. Maybe she was being too hasty, turning him down. After all, Kevin was family. "When you put it like that, you make it hard to turn you down."

A pleased expression took root on his face, growing. "Then don't."

"Okay." There were times, she decided, when it was best for all just to go along with what was happening. She put her hand out. "You've got a deal."

His hand closed over hers. The contact was light, but potent nonetheless. Maybe because he was so acutely aware of her. Slowly he dropped his hand, but his eyes never left her face.

"Last night, when I kissed you," he began slowly, "I was presuming things. Things I shouldn't have without asking—"

They'd already been through this, hadn't they? "Look, I—"

He cut her off. "But I'm asking now. June, I'd like to kiss you. Like to very much." He searched her face, looking for some kind of indication that he wasn't going too far out on a limb here, that he hadn't misread the signs. "But if this makes you uncomfortable in any way—"

She drew her shoulders back. "Talking about it makes me uncomfortable."

"Well, then—" He started to turn to go.

He never made it. June stood up on her toes, her hands going to either side of his face, framing it. "Just shut up and do it," she told him.

And then, before he could, she did. Her lips met his first.

She was also the first to melt.

Melt against him. Melt, period.

It had to do with the heat. But not the kind that was coming from outside. This was a heat that came from within. A heat generated by the very touch of his mouth to hers. By the thoughts that contact created.

And by the longing that appeared instantly.

His arms closed around her, pulling her to him. His body came alive everywhere it touched hers. Kevin could feel flames licking at him, could feel desires coming out of nowhere, assaulting him.

Demanding to be recognized.

To be appeased.

He wanted what he rarely even thought about anymore. He wanted to make love with her.

The thought exploded in his head like a grenade that was on a delayed firing pattern. Stunned, Kevin pulled his head back as if some sudden electrical force had jolted through him.

It took her a second to realize that the kiss was over, that there was air between them instead of the intimate press of flesh. She looked at him in surprise. "What is it?"

"I should be getting back. Now."

He said the last word so urgently, so forcefully, she knew that he had to be feeling the same shock waves through his body that she felt through hers. It was as if her body had been drenched with dew, only to have it sizzle off her skin.

It took her more than a moment to gather herself together.

"Right." She drew a breath, her mind fuzzy. What *was* it that he did to her? "They'll be looking for you," she murmured.

He stepped outside. After the darkness within, late hour or not, there was entirely too much daylight to deal with. He shaded his eyes. "I'll see you tomorrow."

"What time?" she called after him.

One corner of his mouth rose as he crossed back to her. "I thought time didn't matter here."

He had her there. She scrambled for an excuse. "It doesn't, I just—"

Kevin laughed. "I'm only kidding." He wondered if April would mind letting him use her car again. "Nine all right?"

"Half the day's used up by then. If you want to get anything done, you'll have to come earlier." She was only half kidding.

"Earlier then," he promised as he got into April's car.

"Earlier," she murmured, watching him drive away. She stood watching for a long time.

That had been a very vulnerable moment, she thought.

Very slowly, June ran her fingertips along her lips. She could still feel the pressure, still taste him. She knew she should be grateful to Kevin. That had he been someone like Haggerty, or one of the others, he would have used the opportunity to talk her out of her clothes and into a prone position.

Yes, she should be grateful, she thought, her hand dropping to her side.

But all she was, was frustrated.

With a sigh, June went back inside. The screen door slammed against its jamb, announcing her less-than-pleased demeanor.

"Where have you been?" Like a jack-in-the-box, Alison popped up from the chair and flew to her brother's side the moment he walked in through the door. She didn't know whether to laugh or cry. He was supposed to stay at their place tonight and he was very late. "Do you realize I was ready to have Max start combing the area for your body?"

Though he appreciated his sister's concern, from his standpoint, there was no reason to get so upset. "I'm thirty-seven years old, Alison. I've got an uncanny sense of direction and I can take care of myself."

"This isn't downtown Seattle, Kevin. There aren't signs on every corner to help you along your way. People get seriously lost out here. And," she finished dramatically, "turn up seriously dead." When he made no comment, she turned expectantly toward her husband. "Help me out here, Luc. Tell him."

But Luc was content to sit back and let the drama unfold without him. He knew better than to get into the line of fire. He waved her on. "You're doing just fine without me."

"Men," she sighed in disgust. And then her eyes narrowed as she looked at her brother. "You still haven't answered me. Where *were* you?"

He was extremely easygoing, but that wasn't to be mistaken for being a doormat. He'd never been one of those. "Haven't you got the roles reversed a little here? I'm the big brother, you're the little sister." He looked at her pointedly. "The very little sister." Even in heels, which she wasn't wearing, Alison barely came up to his chest.

An accusing glint entered her eyes. "You're evading the question."

Kevin looked over Alison's head toward his brother-in-law. "She's gotten a lot more demanding since she's left home."

Luc chuckled quietly. "This air'll do that to you," he agreed.

Close to the end of her patience, Alison fisted her hands on her hips. "Kev-in."

Luc pretended to take refuge behind his book. "Uh-oh, when she draws your name out like that, you're in trouble. I'd answer her if I were you."

It was never his intention not to answer her, just not to have it come across as if he were enduring the third degree. "I stopped by the farmhouse."

At first, she didn't know what he was talking about. "What farmhouse? The abandoned one?"

He thought that an apt description for the place where June was living. "No, June's, although it might as well have been abandoned." He began to walk out of the room. "Never saw anything before so desperately in need of work that hadn't been condemned by the board of health first—"

Moving quickly, she put herself in front of her brother. He was *not* going to escape this easily. "Back up here, you stopped at June's?"

"I just said that." Glancing toward Luc, Kevin struggled to suppress his grin. He could almost see the questions multiplying in his sister's head. "Keep up, Aly."

She bit back her temper. "I will if you stop jumping around to unimportant things." This definitely had promise. "What were you doing at June's place?"

"Well, for the first few hours I was fixing her tractor."

Alison's brows drew together. She looked toward Luc, but he was proving to be no help whatsoever. She was on her own here. "Is that some kind of euphemism for—"

Kevin almost laughed out loud. "A machine, Alison, I was fixing an antiquated machine so that June could use it on the farm." He looked over her head at Luc again and deadpanned. "Just exactly what is it that you've done to her?"

The expression on Luc's face was the last word in innocence as he continued thumbing through his book. "The nights here are six months long."

Kevin nodded to himself as he started to cross to the threshold again. "That would explain it."

This time, Alison grabbed his arm. "Hold it, mister. I'm not through with you yet. What did you do for the rest of the time you were gone? Dinnertime came and went," she reminded him. "By the way, it's in the refrigerator if you're hungry."

But he shook his head. "June put me to work fixing fence posts. Actual posts," he added, just in case she thought that was a euphemism, too.

"I know that," Alison muttered defensively.

"And then I made her dinner," he concluded. "Except I thought it was lunch. Hard to tell time without a watch up here. I've misplaced mine somewhere.''

''I can lend you one until you find it,'' Luc volunteered. ''I've got an old one I don't use anymore.''

Were they deliberately trying to make her crazy? ''Stop talking about trivial things and let me get this straight,'' Alison demanded. ''You cooked for her?'' Before Kevin could answer, she turned her head toward Luc. ''He cooked for her.'' Did Luc have any idea what that meant, to have her brother actually prepare something for someone? Alone, he was given to making sandwiches. This required effort.

Luc nodded soberly. ''In some third-world countries, that would mean you're practically engaged.'' He sustained a swat from his wife for his trouble.

She turned her attention back to Kevin. ''So that's why you're late? You were cooking for her?'' For the first time since he'd walked in, she smiled at him. ''And then what?''

''And then we ate what I cooked.''

''And then?''

Kevin pretended to think. ''And then we washed dishes.''

She curled her fingers into her hand to keep from strangling her brother. ''And?''

He spread his hands out innocently. ''And then we dried them.''

''Kev-in!''

''She's shouting now,'' Kevin said to Luc. ''Does

that still mean the same thing it did when she was living in Seattle?''

"She's mad."

"It means the same thing."

She knew what they were doing, but she was in no mood to kid around. "Will you two stop talking about me as if you're dealing with a mentally deficient person?" She enunciated her question very slowly. "Kevin, did you kiss her?"

For his part, he had no secrets, but this involved another person and he wasn't about to broadcast her doings, not even to his sister.

"That is my business, Aly." But he hated to see the look of frustrated disappointment that overtook her features. "And even if I did, it doesn't mean anything. June's a member of the family, remember? A kid."

"She's twenty-two," Alison reminded him.

He wasn't about to get into an argument. "Practically a kid," he allowed.

Luc came in, a ready referee. "So, are you seeing the kid again?" The tone in his voice told Kevin he already knew the answer to that.

He nodded, too tired to stretch this out any longer. His muscles were beginning to ache from the day he'd put in. Nothing like honest toil to exhaust you. "Tomorrow. I promised to help fix up her house."

This was going well, Alison thought. Lily was going to be happy. But for the sake of the situation, she knew she had to at least make a stab at some kind of protest. "I thought you were helping Lily with the wedding arrangements."

Kevin looked at Alison. "Does she want me to?" They both knew the answer to that.

"Well, no," Alison admitted, "But—"

"That's what I thought." He rested his case. "That's why I volunteered to do a few things around June's place while I'm here. There's no excuse for her living under conditions like that. Besides, when winter hits, she's liable to freeze to death."

Alison and Luc exchanged looks. Neither one was about to tell him that they had already made plans with the others to hold what was tantamount to a house-raising for June once the wedding was a thing of the past. This was far better.

"Very observant of you to notice," Alison murmured. "But then, nothing ever did get by you." She looked toward the kitchen. "Are you hungry?"

She didn't think June could have had much in the way of food, even taking Kevin's gift for preparation into account. He couldn't have exactly performed the miracle of the loaves and fishes.

"No," he demurred. "But what I am is tired," he admitted. "I think I'll turn in early. Good night." He nodded toward Luc and paused to kiss Alison before heading up the stairs.

"Sweet dreams," Alison called out after him.

He didn't have to turn around to look at her. He could hear the grin in her voice.

Chapter Eight

June stood back a few feet from the front porch and took a long, scrutinizing look at the farmhouse. Kevin had been coming over every day since they'd struck the bargain, applying himself to patching the roof, replacing shingles where they were needed, replacing complete boards where weather and time had eaten through. The sound of hammering and sawing had been a steady companion now for almost two weeks.

He might need to be kept occupied, but she was certainly the one who'd benefited from his labor.

He was painting the outside of the house now and she had to admit she hardly recognized the old building. Kevin looked so intent, she thought as she approached him. And so utterly masculine. There were splotches of paint on him here and there, and some smeared across his chest, laid bare again in deference to the humid weather.

Her fingers itched to rub the paint away from his chest. June pushed her hands deeper into her pockets.

He could feel her watching him. Had felt it for a while now. "Approve?"

Yes! Her eyes lingered on him, on the hard muscles that moved with grace as he transformed dark wood into light, then reluctantly shifted to the building itself again.

"It looks like a completely different house." There was deep admiration in her voice.

Kevin went to dip his brush in again and saw that there was almost nothing left. If he wanted to finish this side before evening, he was going to need to get more paint from town.

He set the paintbrush down and stepped back. So close to his work, all he could see at his present vantage point was a blizzard of white. Because the house could easily be lost in one of the famous snowstorms that hit the area, he'd painted the wood around the windows and the shutters in a brilliant shade of royal blue.

"It's just a matter of putting in a few new boards and giving the place several good coats of paint."

It was decidedly more than that, she thought, looking over his work. It was love, love of a job well-done and she could see it in every stroke, in every new nail he'd driven in.

He was a man, she thought, who didn't do things by half measures. A man who believed in sticking to something until it was finished. A man who gave of himself.

Abruptly June reined herself in before she could get too carried away. Her mother had probably felt the same way about her father. According to her grandmother, Wayne Yearling had had a golden tongue and could have charmed birds right out of their trees even with a cat strolling nearby. She'd heard her father had promised her mother the moon. Utterly enamored, Rose Hatcher had broken her engagement to the man she was about to marry and had run off with Wayne, only to return nine months later with a newborn in her arms and an unemployed husband at her side. Ursula had taken them in, then signed the papers to the deed that gave them title to the farm. A farm that her father had failed to make thrive.

Kevin's not promising you the moon, she told herself. *He's just being helpful.*

There was no comparison between Kevin and her father. Besides, Kevin was adding color to her house, not her life, she insisted silently. He wasn't turning her head with compliments or empty words. If she felt special around him, well, it was nothing that he had set out to do, nothing he'd calculated on. After all, he had no way of knowing just how sexy he looked with white paint sprinkled along the dark hairs of his chest.

She was getting carried away again, June admonished herself. She nodded at his latest handiwork. "You really don't have to do this, you know."

He didn't see it that way. He *needed* to keep busy. "Might as well do something productive while I'm here. Lily made it clear in no uncertain terms that she was going to handle her own wedding arrangements. Something about serving my head on a platter if I got in the way had been bandied about." He grinned. His sister was a despot when it came to planning parties. Even the tea parties she'd held as a child had been carefully orchestrated. That should have been his first clue that he had not so benevolent a dictator on his hands. "I'm not even sure if Max is allowed to give her any input."

"I can't see Max hanging around, waiting to be 'allowed' to do anything." If Max was on the sidelines, it was because he *wanted* to be there. "My brother's quiet, but he's not the kind of man who lets himself be steamrolled over." June tilted her head to the side, as if seeing him for the first time. Or at least exploring a new notion for the first time. "You kind of remind me of him. Except that you're a lot handier than Max ever was." Max didn't know his way around cars beyond the basics and, as far as carpentry went, she wouldn't have wanted to live in a house that he had single-handedly restored.

"I remind everyone of their big brother," Kevin told her.

"I didn't mean that." June looked at him pointedly. "I don't think of you as a big brother."

His eyes held hers. Desire raised its head. "You should."

There were only inches between them. She wanted there to be less. "Why?"

He took the first step. And it was to back away. The moment evaporated. "Because otherwise you've got a half-naked man running around your property with a paintbrush. People'll talk."

She laughed shortly. "People around here always talk. It's their biggest hobby. Cable finally came in a couple of years ago, but it's not all that reliable and besides—" she gestured around "—this is the longest running story in the area."

He thought she meant the farm. Which brought the circle back to her. "You?"

She shook her head. "The town." She thought about what people had said about her when she was younger. "I'm just the no-account's youngest daughter." Some hadn't known what to make of her when she grew older and preferred motor oil to perfume. "The odd one who liked to tinker with engines instead of men." She shrugged. "It's a lot safer that way. For the most part, you can figure your way around an engine.'' Humor curved her mouth, but only partially so as she looked at him. ''Men now are a whole different story.''

He combed the flecks of paint off his chest with his fingers, aware that she was watching his every move. In a moment of truth, he admitted something he didn't generally talk about. ''Funny, I always felt that way about women. Lot more mysteries there than what it take to make an engine purr.''

His choice of words caught her attention. ''You've tried your hand at making women purr?''

He'd only meant it as an expression. ''Not me. Until he got married, that was always Jimmy's department. I wouldn't know where to start.''

She didn't know whether he was being coy, or completely unaware of the effect he had on women. On her. ''Seems to me, kissing would be a good place for you to start. The way you kiss, you could knock the socks off a barefoot woman.''

''Really?'' He looked at her quizzically.

''Really,'' she affirmed.

''I had no idea that you were that experienced.''

She shrugged loftily. ''I've had my share.'' It was a lie, but not one she'd admit readily. ''Besides, you don't have to live in a major city to know a skyscraper when you come across one.''

He was flattered despite himself and laughed. ''You're something else again, June.''

''Am I?'' She was playing with fire and she knew

it, but she couldn't seem to shake herself loose of the heat that was taking hold of her. Drawing her in. "Just what else would you say I was?"

A temptress. A temptress in blue jeans. He tore himself away from the thought and the pervading feeling it generated.

"Well, under those baggy overalls and that shapeless work shirt, and that smudge on your nose—" he paused to wipe it away with his thumb "—is a beautiful woman just waiting to happen."

Because there were still traces of the smudge left, he wiped at it again, more slowly this time, and succeeded in arousing himself even more.

He could feel his heart beating harder, far harder than when he'd been on the roof, in danger of sliding off and splitting his head open. There the danger had been one-sided. Here it came at him from many fronts.

She cocked her head, her eyes never leaving his mouth. "Maybe I've already happened," she said softly.

"Maybe," he agreed, just before he brought his lips down to hers.

And very nearly sealed both their fates.

Like the numbers on the Richter scale, which increased by a thousandfold with each numeric elevation, each kiss seemed to be a thousandfold more potent, more powerful than its predecessor. He felt as if his very world was being rocked.

And in a way it was, because he began entertaining thoughts on a regular basis that would have had no place in his life a few months ago.

That shouldn't have a place in his life now, not when it came to June.

With a few more years between them, she could have easily been his daughter. He wasn't supposed to be having sexual thoughts about someone like that. What the hell was wrong with him?

Putting his hands on her shoulders, Kevin physically moved her back away from him. Surprised entered her face as her eyes slowly focused on him. "That wasn't supposed to happen."

June sighed, not wanting to let go of the moment. Feeling it slip away nonetheless. "Kevin, can't you just do something without debating it? It happened, so it was supposed to happen. And I'm not sorry it did." She looked down at the paint can by his feet. "Is that your last one?"

"What?"

She grinned. "I meant paint can, not kiss." She jerked her thumb in the direction of her vehicle. "Because I can run into town and get more. Paint," she clarified.

He'd already decided to go into town. And now the need was more urgent than before. He needed to put space between them. A whole lot of space. "I'll get the paint. I could use a break right now."

"From the work, or from something else?" She

looked at him knowingly. For a brave man, he certainly didn't act it all the time.

His expression was the soul of innocence. "You're the one who told me not to overcomplicate things, remember?" Kevin picked up his shirt from the railing he'd painted two days ago. Despite the humidity that hung oppressively all around them, the railing had eventually dried.

She knew she shouldn't stare at him like that, but she couldn't help herself. He was one magnificent specimen of manhood. "If you go to the emporium without your shirt on, I guarantee you that Mrs. Kellogg will sell you the paint at cost. Maybe even make you a present of it."

He slipped on the shirt and began rebuttoning it. "And why would she do that?"

"Have you *seen* Mr. Kellogg?"

He laughed, tucking his shirt in. "You really are good for a man's ego."

"I don't say that to every man," she informed him. *I don't say that to any man. Only you.*

He wanted to kiss her again before he left. But if he did, he knew he wasn't going to leave. Not for a very long time.

So, in self-preservation, Kevin merely nodded at her and walked to Alison's Jeep. "I'll be back in a little while," he promised.

She pressed her lips together. Maybe he was right,

maybe they needed some space, some perspective. Every time she was around him, she lost it.

"I might not be here when you get back." June pointed toward the horizon, to where the property continued. "I've got some work waiting for me in the south field."

"I could do that when I come back."

She shook her head. "You're doing too much as it is. I don't want to be accused of wearing you out before the wedding."

"You've got a point." He turned the key in the ignition. Lily's wedding was a little more than a week away. His ticket home was for the day after that.

Time was growing shorter.

The thought filled him with a melancholy that he ordinarily associated with moving through life without his siblings. Which only proved to him that at bottom he viewed June in the same light as he did Alison, Lily and Jimmy. Just another sibling.

And then he shook his head as he turned the Jeep toward Hades. Funny the lies people told themselves just to continue.

There were times when she liked to come to the grave site by herself and just talk things out with her mother. That there was no audible response never troubled her too much. If she was very quiet, she could feel the response in her heart.

This was one of those times.

She bit her lip, debating. She really did have work to do. Hay didn't take care of itself.

The debate was short-lived.

On impulse, June abandoned her work and stopped to pick a handful of wildflowers that seemed to have grown expressly for the purpose of decorating her mother's grave. They were wild roses. Her mother had always loved wild roses.

It was what her father had called her. Wild Rose.

June placed the freshly plucked bouquet on the seat beside her and drove toward the town's small cemetery. She needed to be near her mother. To share a moment in time the way she hadn't been able to in life.

The cemetery contained the remains of all the past citizens of Hades who had come here in search of something, or to flee something. The former had been the case for the two oldest bodies buried on the hill, that of two miners. They had been the original founders of the small town, one of whom had given the town its name in a fit of despair and desperation. He'd thought of it as hell, but society being what it had been in those days, he'd called it by the only acceptable label that could have been given then: Hades. It had stuck and aroused a kind of dry humor when referred to in the dead of bone-chilling winter.

She'd always been amused by that story, June thought as she approached the small wrought-iron-gated area.

Her smile faded a little as she saw that she wasn't going to be alone here, the way she'd hoped. There was someone else there at the cemetery already. His back to her, he stood over a grave.

She didn't recognize the coat.

The town's population was still small enough for her to be able to recognize not only all the inhabitants of Hades, but also the clothing they wore.

Maybe Mr. Kellogg was carrying a new line of winter apparel at the emporium. The coat looked too warm for this time of year.

She stopped the car and took measure of the person she deemed a stranger.

The man was tall, with flowing iron-gray hair. Though he was broad shouldered, his shoulders seemed to be slumped, as if life had beaten him down year by year, inch by inch.

A relative? A curious stranger absorbing the names of past citizens for some unknown reason of his own? They had a few tourists here in the summer, but this wasn't exactly a tourist draw.

Taking her key from the ignition, June got out of the vehicle.

Strangers were supposed to invite caution, but she had never been the cautious type. Especially since, she realized, the man stood over the very grave she wanted to put her flowers on.

What was he doing here?

There were flowers on the grave already. Fresh

ones. The wilt of even a day's separation from the soil hadn't begun to penetrate the blooms. Had Max or April had the same inclination today? Neither one had mentioned intending to come here.

Maybe her grandmother had passed by. She tried to remember if today had some sort of significance. And then she remembered.

It was her mother's wedding anniversary.

She stared at the stranger's back. Had he put the flowers there?

Why?

The word echoed in her head as her stomach tightened instinctively in anticipation. A strange numbness descended over her.

She strode forward. "That's my mother's grave," she announced crisply. The man's head jerked up in response, as if he hadn't heard her approach. "What are you doing here?"

His hands were working the rim of a shapeless tan hat, a fedora that had seen better decades. "Saying I'm sorry," he replied quietly, addressing his words to the body beneath the soil.

June could feel her spine stiffening. "Why would you be sorry? You didn't know her." There was a stillness in the air, not even the sound of an insect whizzing by. Nothing. Only the words hung there between them. "Did you?"

"Yes. For a little while." Each word was slowly

measured out, like precious drops of water in the desert. "She was my wife."

June raised her chin, anger and defiance warring within her for control even as her voice remained steely. "That's not possible. She was only married once. And he's dead."

Eyes that had seen too much now looked at her. "April?"

She glared at him, stubborn, hostile. Damning him. "No."

Recognition flooded him. She'd grown so much. How many years had gone by? He'd lost them all and lost count. "June."

"Process of elimination?" Sarcasm wrapped itself around each word. "Simple enough, I suppose." This was her father. Her father had returned. Why the hell had he done that now, when it no longer meant anything? When her mother could no longer fling herself into his arms and dampen his shirt with her joy? "You couldn't very well say Max, now could you?"

His eyes swept over her, drinking in the sight. Tears stood still, shimmering against an intense field of blue. She had his eyes, but everything else belonged to Rose. "My God, June, you look just like her. Just like your mother." His voice almost broke. "She was such a beautiful woman."

"Not after all the life had been drained out of her," June retorted coldly. She wanted to scream things at him, to tell him how horrible he was for leaving them all, for leaving her mother and condemning her to a life of sorrow until she completely wasted away. "What are you doing here, now? Run out of places to see?"

He tried to draw himself up but couldn't. It was as if the weight of his transgressions had permanently bent him. "I came back to say I'm sorry."

"Won't do you any good." June deliberately stooped down and picked up the flowers he had placed there, then tossed them aside. She replaced them with her own. "She can't hear you."

He knew it was too late for that. But not too late for everything. Not yet. "But you can. You and April and Max."

"Just because you have ears doesn't mean you can hear." Her eyes narrowed accusingly as she looked at him. He hardly looked like the man in the photograph her grandmother kept. The man there had been laughing. It was his wedding day, his and her mother's. She didn't remember ever seeing her mother smile that way. Her expression had been one of hope. "You didn't. She begged you to stay and you didn't hear her."

He rubbed his hand over his face, searching for explanations to things he could no longer even explain to himself. "You were too young to understand."

"But April wasn't." Her sister had been eleven when their father had left them. And, in her own way, just as shattered as their mother had been by the event. But only April had rallied, because she needed to take care of them as their mother drifted away from reality. "Grandmother wasn't. And they told me that my mother begged you not to leave. *Begged you.* And you left anyway. Said you felt as if this town was strangling you. And that we didn't matter."

"I never said that," he protested, trying to take her arm.

She pulled away. "You didn't have to. Actions always speak louder than words, especially up here." She started to walk away, not wanting to share this hallowed ground with him. "And your actions spoke volumes."

"June, wait, I want to make it up to you. To you and the others. What can I do?"

It wasn't until she was back in her vehicle again that she gave him an answer.

"Leave."

Chapter Nine

June wasn't at the farmhouse when he returned with the extra containers of white paint he'd picked up in town. But she'd already told him she might not be, so he didn't think anything of it at first.

It was only when he climbed back up on the ladder again, and his view of the surrounding area was much wider, that he began to wonder about her whereabouts. The tractor was exactly where she'd left it when she'd returned to the house late yesterday. If she wasn't using the tractor, what was she doing?

As the question occurred to him, Kevin shook his head. There had to be a hundred different things that needed doing around a farm. She could be busy with any one of them. Not having been raised on a farm himself, he had no idea exactly what she was busy with or where.

And he had no idea why an uneasy feeling kept buzzing around in his head.

He was just a born worrier, he supposed. At least, that was what Lily had called him. Stretching, he reached over to a section he'd missed earlier.

He hadn't always been a worrier, he thought. Growing up in Seattle, he'd been as carefree as they came, making plans for himself and the life he was sure was ahead of him, ripe for the taking. He'd wanted something to do with medicine, to be a surgeon and practice in a teeming metropolis, occasionally traveling to third-world nations to help people who would otherwise never even see their twenties without a doctor.

A smile teased his lips as he began painting another board he'd recently replaced. He supposed he and Jimmy Stewart had a lot in common that way, at least, the character Stewart had played in *It's A Wonderful Life*. Planning one life, leading another.

Nothing had gone according to plan for him, not since his parents had both died within such a short period of time of each other. Rather than attending college with an eye out for medical school, he'd gone to work instead. He'd taken a few courses at night when time permitted and gotten a two-year degree in business to help him eventually take over and run the cab service that had allowed him to put food on the table for his siblings.

They were right—whoever had said that life was something that happened while you were making plans. His had happened while he shelved his own plans.

He didn't make plans anymore. There was no real point. The three people he'd been providing for were providing for themselves now, and living their own lives.

No, no more plans, he thought, climbing down one rung, but damn, he had to do something with himself once this vacation was over.

He let his mind drift as he worked. Maybe he'd buy into that home security business he'd been looking into, when he got back to Seattle. Security at home was the kind of thing that was right up his alley, anyway.

Kevin started seriously considering it.

The sound of an engine approaching caught his attention and pulled him out of his mental wanderings.

At first, he thought it might be a plane flying low overhead. Shayne or Sydney making a quick run to Anchorage for one reason or another. But nothing was moving in the sky other than a flock of birds.

The engine roar was coming from a car. Looking round, he quickly zeroed in on the source. June swiftly approached the house, driving far faster than it seemed necessary.

From his vantage point, it looked as if she was going over eighty miles an hour.

She was coming from the general direction of the town. Something had happened. There was no other explanation for the sudden speed. The thought barely registered as Kevin scrambled down the ladder, paint splashing over the side of the can. The container almost tipped over as he hurriedly set it on the ground.

Running toward her, he saw that June's face was the color of ashes.

Something *had* happened. He didn't even want to speculate on what.

June brought the vehicle to a skidding stop less than two feet away from him. But instead of getting out, she remained sitting behind the wheel.

She was trembling, he realized.

At her side, Kevin was afraid to touch her. Her expression was like something he'd never seen before. Disoriented, lost.

"June, what happened? You're shaking like a leaf."

After she'd driven away from her father, the whole situation began to appear almost surreal to her, as if it couldn't possibly have been true. Her father was dead, she'd been so sure of that. In her heart, she knew that was what April and Max believed.

Could she have hallucinated the whole thing? Hallucinations weren't uncommon in places like this, but they were usually the result of severe cabin fever, or being lost in the wild for several days. At the very least, a high fever came into play.

And she had neither.

Trying to focus, to shake off the feeling that was struggling for control over her, she heard Kevin's voice somewhere in the distance.

"June?"

Somehow, she'd gotten out of the Jeep. Whether Kevin had lifted her out or she had climbed out on her own, she wasn't sure.

The only thing she knew was that she didn't want it to be true. She didn't want her father to be back. Not after all this time, not after she'd buried him in her mind years ago.

"June, what's wrong?" He curbed the urge to try to shake her out of the daze she seemed to be in. "Did something happen in town? To you? To the others?" A dozen different things occurred to him. He refused to flesh any of them out until she gave him something to work with. "June." His voice was urgent, even as it was soft, kind. "Talk to me, I can't help you unless you talk to me."

Desperate, Kevin thought of calling the clinic and having Jimmy drive out. From his limited medical knowledge, he thought that June looked as if she was in shock.

Had she gotten hurt? Been in a car accident?

Quickly he checked her limbs to make sure there weren't any injuries not readily visible at first glance.

But there were no cuts, no bruises. Nothing except the haunted look in her eyes.

As if she'd seen something she didn't want to.

At a loss, Kevin picked her up in his arms to carry her into the house. It was then that she came to. With a small cry, she began to resist, pushing against his chest. "No!"

Had someone tried to attack her? He had a thousand questions and not a single answer.

"All right." Kevin put her down on the ground again, trying to think of what to do.

He had no idea what was going on or why she was behaving this way, only that he wasn't about to leave her until he had some kind of answer and she was herself again.

Carefully pushing back a strand of hair that had fallen into her face, he peered at her. The color wasn't returning.

"You feel up to telling me what's going on?"

Slowly her eyes turned toward him, as if she hadn't really been aware that it was him who'd been talking to her. "He's back."

"Who's back?"

Kevin thought of Haggerty, the man who'd tried to corner her at the Salty the other night. But the miner didn't seem like the type to force himself beyond a point. And even so, he had every confidence in the world that June could hold her own against someone like that. This was something more. Something far more serious.

"Take your time," he said softly, belying the impatience he felt. Whatever was going on had taken its toll on her. He wasn't about to add to that by demanding she talk to him before she was ready.

June swallowed before she answered, the words sticking to the roof of her mouth, glued there by sheer disbelief.

Why? Why now?

"My father," she whispered hoarsely. "My father's back."

He knew all about the story, had gotten it not just in bits and pieces from her, but from Jimmy and Lily as well. The story of the man who couldn't stay put, who'd created a family only to abandon it, sacrificing it on the altar of his wanderlust. Everyone in town believed that he was gone for good, most likely dead.

"Are you sure?"

Her eyes darted to his face, anger leaping into him. He took no offense.

"Of course I'm sure. Don't you think I know what my own father looks like?" she lashed out, then instantly regretted it. She pressed her lips together. "I'm sorry, I'm just—"

He cut her short. "You don't have to apologize. I'd feel just as shaken up as you in your place." He spoke slowly, softly, not wanting her to fall apart. He'd gotten to know her pretty well in the past two weeks and had never seen her like this. She seemed so completely vulnerable. "Where did you see him?"

She shut her eyes for a moment. The image was burned into her mind. "At the cemetery." She looked at Kevin. The pain that assaulted her was overwhelming. Why? It shouldn't matter anymore. It should have stopped mattering a long time ago. She thought it had. "He was standing over my mother's grave."

That would explain why the tractor hadn't been moved. "Is that where you were just now?"

June nodded. She looked off in the general direction of Cemetery Hill. "I go there sometimes," she told him quietly, almost talking to herself. "To talk." Realizing what she'd just said, she flushed. "Just to clear my head. You probably think that's crazy."

He smiled at her, refraining from taking her into his arms the way he wanted to. "No. I talk to mine all the time. They both wanted to be cremated, so there's no actual grave to go to. Their ashes were scattered. In a way, I guess you might say they're all around me. Kind of with me all the time."

She looked at him, gratitude burrowing its way in between the walls of shock that had closed in around her. He understood, she thought. It meant a great deal right now to have someone understand.

"Did he recognize you?"

She laughed shortly. "He thought I was April. And then he said I looked just like my mother." She dragged her hand restlessly through her hair. He noted with relief that some measure of color finally returned to her face. "He was just—there." Her eyes searched his as if she needed him to understand. "Like it was all right. Like he hadn't ever gone away."

"What did he want?" Kevin asked gently.

She began to move around. He shadowed her steps, afraid that she might faint without warning. "To make everything crazy."

That had been accomplished, he thought. "What did he say, exactly?"

Turning away from him, she tilted her head up toward the sky, blinking. Determined not to let the tears spill out. If you cried, it meant that you were weak, and she'd always been strong. Strong, just like April and Max and her grandmother.

She drew in a breath, composing herself. "That he was sorry."

Kevin knew how small a word that could sound like. And how much it could really contain. But now wasn't the time to take the side of a man who'd wounded her so badly. "He apologized for leaving?"

She clenched her hands into fists at her side as she swung around to face him. Her feelings were all over the map. Sadness, anger, confusion, they were all jumbled up inside of her.

"He tried to." Her mouth grew bitter. "My mother's dead because of him and he's *sorry*," she spit out. "He thinks that if he comes back and says that, everything's going to be all right. That everything's forgiven.'' Anger flashed in her blue eyes as she looked up at him. ''Well, it's *not*.''

He could only guess at what she was feeling, but he did his best. ''I know, June, I know. It's going to take time.''

''There's not that much time in the world.''

She couldn't quell the bitterness that was taking hold inside her, the emotion that was the flip side of all the love she'd felt for her father as a child. He'd ruined it, ruined her perfect world, taken away her childhood before she had ever had a chance to use it. Before she'd had a chance to store it away.

Kevin placed a gentling hand on her shoulder. ''I know you feel that way now—''

June shrugged him off angrily. ''I'll always feel that way,'' she countered, moving away from him. ''A couple of words offered up years too late aren't going to change that.''

This was a great deal for her to take in all at once, Kevin thought. He appreciated that she was in the middle of an emotional earthquake, but she needed to calm down. If her father had really returned, she needed to begin the business of forgiving. For her own sake.

''Where is he now?''

She thought a moment, setting the jumbled scenario in order. ''He's staying at Luc's hotel.''

Her father had called out the information to her as she'd driven away. She hadn't wanted to hear him, but she couldn't help it. He'd raised his voice over the roar of her engine.

She had no idea if he meant to stay here in Hades. The younger Wayne Yearling couldn't wait to leave the confines of Hades, but her father was older now, and somehow smaller and far less robust than the man she'd looked at so many times in the wedding photograph.

Her eyes widened as more thoughts crowded into her head, making her realize the possible consequences of her father's sudden reappearance.

She clutched at Kevin's arm. "We've got to get him to leave." Her voice rose excitedly. "He'll ruin Max's wedding. He'll—"

"I can talk to him if you want," Kevin told her. Though it wasn't his place, he could ask the man to leave her alone, at least for the time being, until she got used to the idea that he was back. Until she could find it in her heart to begin to forgive him. "But I think Max and April need to know about this."

"No." She was adamant, and as protective of hers as he was of his. "It's not fair to put them through this." It was enough that she had experienced the shock of seeing her father alive and here. She didn't want that for her brother and sister.

"You can't make that decision for them, June. They might want to hear him out." Kevin understood where she was coming from, from the very best place in her heart.

"Why?" she demanded, turning on him, feeling betrayed all over again. She'd expected him of all people to understand, to back her up, not take her father's side. "So he can spin some more of his lies for them? So that he can make more promises he's not going to keep?" She shook her head, rejecting the idea. "You weren't there. You didn't see my mother or my sister after he left. He broke hearts, Kevin," she insisted, trying to make him understand. "He doesn't deserve to have them anymore."

"No, you're probably right, he probably doesn't deserve to have them back. But it's still a decision that April and Max have to make on their own. You owe them that." She opened her mouth to argue with him, but he cut her off. He knew exactly what was going on in her head. "I know you just want to protect them, but you can't. And you can't punish your father for all four of you. You can just hold back yourself."

"I'm not trying to punish him," she cried. Her words echoed back to her and she sighed. "All right, maybe I am. But why shouldn't I?" she demanded heatedly. "He deserves it. All he had to do was just stay and everything would have been all right."

It was easy, from the vantage point of hindsight, to spin a perfect scenario. But life was seldom perfect. He knew that better than most. "Maybe not."

She released a breath, trying to keep from lashing out at him again. He wasn't the target, he was just standing in the way. Making sense at a time when she didn't want to have anything to do with sense. When she just wanted to vent.

"Well, we'll never know, will we?"

"No," he agreed quietly, "we won't, and we can debate this until the cows come home and it still won't make any difference." He looked at her pointedly. "What makes a difference is that he's here and you and your brother and your sister are each going to have to deal with that in your own way."

Suddenly she was drained and so very tired. "I don't want to deal with it now."

She raised her head up to him and he saw that there were tears shimmering in her eyes. His heart constricted within his chest. At a moment like this, fairly or not, he could have readily done battle with her father for her.

"I don't want to deal with it now," she repeated, her voice almost breaking.

"Then don't," he whispered.

Kevin took her into his arms and she let him, burying her face in his chest until she could regain control. Something that seemed very far out of reach right now. She hated herself like this, hated the fact that she was weak and that her father could still affect her this way. She was supposed to be above that. She wasn't supposed to care if he lived or died or showed up here. None of that was supposed to matter anymore.

So why did it?

Why was there this awful ache inside her? This restless, disoriented feeling that she didn't know what to do with?

Her face against him, she sighed heavily. "Why did he have to show up now?"

Her breath was warm as it traveled along his chest. He was having trouble remembering that his sole function right now was to comfort her, not to feel anything himself, other than empathy.

It wasn't easy.

"I don't think there could have ever been a good time, June."

He was right, she thought. It still didn't make it easier.

"No, but it would had to have been better than now. Max is really happy for maybe the first time in a long time. I don't want anything to spoil that." She raised her head and looked at Kevin, searching his face for a promise she needed. "Please don't tell him that our father's back."

In all good conscience, he didn't feel he could make that promise. "June—"

"Please," she begged, "don't tell him. I'll tell him when I think the time's right."

He didn't know whether he believed her, and it was against his better nature to withdraw like this. Her family was now his family—it had been ever since

Jimmy had married April. But his heart went out to her.

"All right, I won't tell," he promised. "But I think you should warn Max. Warn him and April and your grandmother before your father approaches them. He didn't come back to stay in the shadows."

She sighed deeply. He was right. Suddenly she felt lost and small. "Hold me, Kevin. Just hold me. I'm not sure I can stand up on my own."

"I'll hold you," he told her. "I'll hold you for as long as you want me to." His arms closed around her more tightly. "And I'll talk to your father for you if you want."

She pressed her face against his chest, drawing strength from his warmth. Wishing she could vanish for a little while, until all of this was sorted out. "You'll tell him to go away?"

"If that's what you want."

"You really are a knight in shining armor, aren't you?"

He could feel her smile as it crept along her lips and pressed itself against his chest.

"Maybe not shining, and probably not even a knight—" he kissed the top of her head "—but I'm here for you if you need me."

"I need you," she whispered.

Chapter Ten

Her eyes were saying things to his heart that he was afraid to acknowledge. It led to places Kevin knew he wasn't supposed to go.

"I need you, Kevin," she whispered again.

He couldn't help himself.

There were a thousand different things he could have done in response.

He did only one.

Framing her face as if it were the most precious of treasures, he tilted June's head up to his and pressed his lips against hers.

He meant to do it lightly, gently, to assure her that he was here for her for as long as she needed. But the urgency with which the words were uttered broke through, tearing down the last of his own defenses.

June wrapped her arms around his neck and kissed him back. Hard. Kissed him with all the swirling emotions that had been cut loose by the reappearance of her father in her life, by the catapulting of her very being into a cataclysmic abyss. She needed something to cling to, something stable to anchor her before she was lost to this darkness that was assailing her.

She chose him.

And held on for dear life.

He felt drained. He felt invigorated. And most of all, he felt airborne. Sailing full tilt into a place that had been beckoning to him ever since the first time he'd kissed her.

It was then, during that first kiss, that all the needs he'd put aside, all the emotions he thought had been anesthetized until they'd faded out of existence, had come alive and moved up to the front of the line, waiting for the moment they could be released.

She couldn't think. Down was up, out was in, everything seemed completely jumbled except for the most important thing. That she wanted this, needed this.

Needed him.

Right now, above all else, she needed him, needed this mad whirl he was responsible for that was going on in her head, going faster and faster until it stole her very breath away.

She felt the kiss deepening and wasn't entirely sure of her part in that, only of her reaction to it.

He made her feel drunk with power, with excitement and so very safe she could have cried.

Barriers were breaking down within him like fences built out of ice facing the full power of the summer sun. He caught hold of himself before it was too late. Before he couldn't.

"June—"

But she wouldn't let him say anything more. This time, it was she who framed his face, she who kissed him, blotting out the words of caution, of protest she was afraid were coming.

"Don't talk," she begged him. "Just make love with me."

Make love with me.

The invitation rose up, twelve feet high, before him. But rather than give in to the raging inferno that was singeing his very insides, Kevin forced himself to step back. He caught June by the shoulders, holding her in place.

"I'm not going to let you do something you're going to regret just because you're upset." It cost him more than she would ever know to say this to her.

"I'm not upset," June insisted. The intensity of her voice lowered as she added, her voice thick with emotion, "And I'm not ever going to regret this."

He knew better. He was too old for her. "That's what you say now—"

She wasn't going to have him use that damn logic of his to ruin this.

"That's what I *mean* now. Are you going to make me beg?" Tears shimmered in her eyes, tears that caught the sun, going straight into his heart as if they rode on a laser beam. "Because I won't beg, Kevin. I—"

Unable to resist the power of her tears, unable to turn away from her, and himself, any longer, Kevin brought his mouth down to hers.

A rapture seized them, until the kiss burned into both their souls.

Still kissing her, Kevin picked her up in his arms again.

This time, she didn't push him away, didn't resist. This time she surrendered herself completely to him, because it was what she wanted. To be his. To have him be hers. Everything else didn't matter.

Feeling his way around, Kevin entered the farmhouse using the rear door. The music from the radio she always left on followed them as he slowly made his way through the kitchen.

When he stopped kissing her, June moaned. Her limbs had been reduced to the consistency of churned butter and she was afraid that he was going to try to argue with her again. She could hardly pull two words together in her brain.

Drawing air into her oxygen-depleted lungs, she slowly blew out a breath, then said, "What?"

"Your bedroom?"

He was asking directions. He was a rare man, indeed.

Kevin saw the smile that curved her lips enter her eyes as she pointed toward the front of the house.

"That way," she breathed.

Knowing he shouldn't, having no choice, Kevin went in the direction she'd indicated.

"You know," he told her, "you should eat occasionally." He felt he was carrying nothing. "The paint cans weighed more."

June curled her body into him, glorying in the heat she felt radiating from him. "What I lack in weight I make up in staying power," she murmured.

Her whole body tingled with anticipation. He'd leeched the sadness out of her, the sorrow that had threatened to drown her, replacing it with a desire so intense she didn't think she could draw a deep breath without feeling it consume her.

He smiled down at her and she could feel the effects of his expression right down to her very core. "No argument there."

"Finally," she breathed.

She meant the single word to encompass both his verbal surrender and the fact that they had reached her bedroom. It was the larger of the two, though not by much. It had been her parents' bedroom once. It had taken her several weeks before she'd decided to use it instead of remaining in the one she'd shared with her siblings.

The latter was smaller, but here at least the memories had been mostly happy ones. She wasn't certain what she'd feel in the room that her parents had slept in. Loved in. It had taken her a while to settle in with the ghosts.

And now she discovered that one of the ghosts was still among the living.

No, she wasn't going to go there, she upbraided herself. Not now, not when she was going to finally make love with Kevin. The way she realized that she'd always wanted to. Maybe that was why she'd always kept everyone else at arm's distance. Because she'd been waiting for someone like him.

And maybe she was just being vulnerable right now, but she didn't want to explore it. She just wanted to feel it. To feel that excitement she knew had to be there rushing through her veins.

"Stop," she ordered softly.

He was certain she'd changed her mind. He stopped dead in his tracks. He looked at her and was surprised when, instead of pushing herself out of his arms, she raised her head to his and kissed him.

And took away the doubts he harbored.

As he crossed the threshold into June's room, he was barely aware of his surroundings. There was precious little to take in. Like the rest of the house, it had an economy of furnishings, an abundance of dis-

array. She was no better a housekeeper in her bedroom than she was in the rest of the house.

He wasn't looking for a housekeeper. Just the
keeper of his soul.

He welcomed a little disorder. His life, he decided,
had been far too orderly. Too restricted. Because even
now, it was tugging at him, warning him of the steps
he was taking and their consequences.

But his blood was too hot and rushing too loudly
for him to take heed any longer.

Very gently, Kevin laid her on her bed.

The blue-and-white down comforter was already
half off the bed and she pushed it aside, letting it fall
to the floor. She lay there, waiting for him. Her eyes
reached out to him in a silent invitation.

He had no idea where he found the strength to
make her a final offer. "Last chance to back out."

Even as he said it, his gut tightened, afraid she'd
listen to him at the very last moment. Afraid June
would come to her senses the way he no longer could
come to his.

She lay there a long moment, just looking at him.
He had no idea what she was thinking. "I'm not going anywhere," she whispered.

It was all he needed to hear.

Stripping off his shirt, he threw it aside onto the
comforter that had sagged to the floor. His eyes never
left hers as he came to her. Kevin slipped his hand

underneath her blouse, softly skimming along the delicate skin he found there.

Her heart pounding, she took his hand and slowly moved it to her breast. Her breath caught, trapped by the look in his eyes as she felt his hand cover her.

He could feel her heart hammering. Keeping time with his, he thought.

His mouth came down to hers again.

Kevin kissed her over and over again, melting them both even as the fire rose higher, demanding more from each.

Consuming both.

She almost tore her shirt from her body, wanting to feel his hands all over her. Wanting to feel that final, infinite surge in her veins, the one that promised to wash everything else from her.

Her fingers were fumbling, getting in each other's way.

"Easy," he whispered against her hair. "Easy."

With patient fingers, he undid the rest of the buttons on her work shirt, guiding the material from her breasts, from her shoulders, until it fell away completely. Her skin was like cream, soft and tempting. He struggled to keep his mind focused on putting her pleasure above his own. He pressed a warm, teasing kiss to the swell above her breasts as he undid the hook at the back of her bra.

She shrugged out of the lacy affair. He caressed

every newly exposed inch of her, making her shiver in anticipation.

Needs she'd never known before came racing to the fore, clamoring for more. Clamoring for fulfillment. Making her yearn.

For pleasure.

For him.

She began fumbling with the button on his jeans, unable to release it.

His soft laugh echoed in her head as Kevin moved her hand away and undid the button himself.

He saw the look in her eyes. She thought he was laughing at her, he realized. Maybe even patronizing her.

Nothing could have been further from the truth. He was enjoying her. Reveling in the wonder of her.

Kevin buried his face in the slope of her neck, breathing in the fragrance of her hair, of her skin. It made his senses swirl at a dizzying speed.

Swiftly he undid the button on her jeans, sliding the denim along her hips. Her underwear rode down with it.

And then she was completely nude, completely pliant before him.

He'd never seen anything so beautiful before in his life, not even inside a museum. Not even in his wildest dreams.

He had no business being here, but it was far too late for warnings to be issued, much less heeded. He wanted her so badly he knew with an unshakable certainty that he'd incinerate if he couldn't have her.

An urgency rushed through her like a bullet train overdue for its destination. And she was overdue, so overdue for what she anticipated was waiting for her at the end of the line.

June pushed the rough fabric from his hips, reveling in the smooth feel of his skin beneath her heated hands. Her pulse pounded as she drove the material down to his knees.

Kevin kicked his jeans and underwear aside and pulled her on top of him. As she squealed in surprise, he kissed the space between her breasts, then turned his attention to each one individually. Swirling his tongue along each of her nipples.

He heard her moan as his blood pumped harder through his veins. His hands braced against her, Kevin moved her so that her torso trailed along his. Hardened him. Moistening her.

Suddenly reversing their positions, he continued his odyssey, kissing the flat of her stomach, curve of her navel and slowly, achingly, moving just beyond a microinch at a time.

Her eyes flew open. June caught hold of his shoulders, digging in her fingers and crying out something unintelligible as he found his way to her inner core. He entered slowly, deliberately, brushing his tongue so that there were rainbows and stars dancing through her brain at the same time, eclipsing one another.

Creating a fire like she'd never felt before.

Twisting, turning, June cried out his name like some wild prayer as she felt herself suddenly driven up over a crest she hadn't even known was there.

And as she sank down, panting, she felt another beginning to rise.

Trying to brace herself, she fisted her hands in his hair. The explosion that racked her came far faster than the first. It left her drenched, exhausted and completely cradled in the arms of wonder.

What was he doing to her? How was he creating this bittersweet ecstasy that made her want to sing one second and cry the next?

And then he worked his way down, kissing her thighs, the hollow behind her knees, moving ever forward until he was at her instep, all the while evoking sensations that had been completely foreign to her, sensations only half hoped for, dreamed of.

She could merely moan and scramble inwardly in an attempt to absorb every new sensation, every new wave of passion, of desire as it came over her.

Moving down one limb, Kevin began the journey back up along the other until he was over her again, covering her mouth with his own.

Covering her body with his.

She felt was if she'd been branded. Exhausted but excited. Aware but anticipating.

She was all things and they all existed because of him.

The look in her eyes empowered him and made him feel humble at the same time. He felt as if he'd been reborn in this small room and could just as easily have died there as well with no complaint.

He'd never felt so alive, so vital and so beholding all at once.

But his energy was ebbing out of his reach. He'd been concentrating all this time on holding himself back just a little longer, wanting to give her pleasure for yet another moment.

A man could wait only so long, hold back only so much. Just the way she took in her breath, moving against him, aroused him almost to the point of no return.

And now, he was out of time.

So, his mouth sealed to hers, Kevin moved himself into position, then drew his head back one last time to look at her. To seal this one precious memory in his brain for all time.

The outline of her lips was blurred from the force of his. He had no idea why that hopelessly excited him, but it did. So much so that he knew he had to have her.

Now.

She seemed to read his mind, or perhaps the needs slamming into her were the same ones hammering away at him.

She opened beneath him, and then, as he moved to enter, she placed her fingers over him, guiding him inside her. He felt his blood surging, felt himself growing harder.

Her eyes never left his.

She moaned as he began to enter.

The realization telegraphed itself to him a single instant before it was too late for him to do anything about it.

June was a virgin.

Chapter Eleven

Instincts told him to back away, as hard as that would have been.

But intense needs elbowed out instincts, fueled by the way June was urgently moving against him, urging him on. Making him want her with every fiber of his being. Making him believe down to the core of his very soul that she wanted him.

He didn't back away.

She cried out when he penetrated her, a soft whimper echoing against his mouth. A whimper that would indelibly remain with him.

Conscience reared up.

But contrition was pushed aside by the way she

clung to him. As if only he could repair whatever damage had been done. The irony of that wasn't lost on Kevin, even in the frenzied heat of the moment.

He made love to her as gently as he was able.

It hurt, but then, she'd known it would. Everything of meaning in life hurt. And he'd already given her so much pleasure, so much more than she'd expected.

June wrapped herself around him as he brought her to that special place where lovers went, that place she'd only imagined was real. The place where she now was.

The wild wave took hold of her, throwing her from the highest of heights, making her feel as if she could fly on a breeze. Holding Kevin to her as tightly as she could because she knew that once he released her, there would only be the ground to face.

A bittersweetness filled Kevin as he raised his head to look at her.

He was angry. Not at her, but for her. Because he'd taken something precious from her when he had no right to. He'd robbed her of her first time.

Rolling off, he stared at the ceiling for a moment. It needed work. So did the situation. "Why didn't you tell me?"

The accusation made her wince inwardly, even as defiance took hold of her entire body. "Tell you what?"

He could hear the hurt beneath the retort. He was

responsible for that. "You know what, that you were a virgin."

Her eyes slanted toward him. "Would you have made love with me if I had?"

"No."

June took a deep breath before she answered, pulling up a sheet that had been crumpled at her feet, and carefully covering herself with it. "Then that's why I didn't tell you."

He sighed, not knowing where to begin, knowing that he couldn't undo the damage. Wishing he'd never come here and at the same time knowing if he hadn't, he would have missed something wonderful. But that was selfish of him.

"June, your first time…it's supposed to be special."

Was this about him? Or her? She felt herself softening as she looked at the man. He wasn't complaining that he'd wasted time with an inexperienced virgin, he was concerned that it hadn't been worthy of her. Was this man real, or just something she'd dreamed up? "What makes you think it wasn't?"

"Because—" He hunted for the right words. When they didn't come, he used what he had. "Because it wasn't with someone your own age." Someone who could give her a future, he added silently. Someone with whom she could *have* a future.

She searched his face. He didn't understand, did he? Didn't understand just how very special he was.

"That wouldn't have made it special. That would have made it the norm." She slid back down against the bed, the fire of confrontation having gone out of her. "If I'd wanted the norm, I would have given in to Haggerty, or Haley, or any one of a number of guys who raised and lowered their brows and said they could take me on a fast trip to paradise."

He couldn't help the laugh that came to his lips. "They really said that?"

Her bare shoulder moved against the mattress in a half shrug. "More or less. Most men aren't exactly romantics up here." She raised herself up on one elbow. "The point is, I knew that I'd know when that person I wanted to be 'the first' came along." She looked at him significantly. "And I did."

She gave him far too much credit. He was certain that the fact that she'd had no father when she'd been growing up had a great deal to do with this image she had of him.

"June—"

She placed a finger to his lips to silence any protest. Protests only ruined things. She was quick to throw a blanket over them.

"Don't worry, Kevin, there aren't any strings. I don't expect or want any. I know you're going back to Seattle after the wedding. And I'm going back to my life—" she grinned broadly "—a little more educated than before you came."

She'd opened up a whole new world to him. He

wasn't a monk, but he knew a miracle when he'd experienced it. "I'm probably the one who's gotten the education."

Her eyes shone as she looked up at him. She knew he was being kind, but she loved the thought that she'd rocked his world a little just the same.

"Really?"

The tempest was gone, the calm returned. And temptation rose on the winds again. Kevin tucked her close against him. "Really. But you still should have told me."

June looked very solemn as she nodded her head. "Kevin?"

He kissed the top of her head, wondering whether she knew just how much she'd affected him. "Yes?"

"I'm a virgin." And then she grinned. "Or was."

It still wasn't a joke to him. He knew that there were men who reveled in being someone's first, but he didn't. At least, not for the sake of merely being the first. Still, it meant a great deal to him. "June—"

"Well, now that you've done the damage—" her eyes teased him as she turned her body toward his in a blatant invitation "—don't you want to do it again?"

Heaven help him, but he did.

He let his hand trail along the soft curve of her frame. "Yes."

She tilted her head up to his. "Well, then? What are you waiting for?"

Certainly not an excuse to get in the way.

With a possessiveness that was completely foreign to him, Kevin brought his mouth down to hers.

"Not a thing."

Behind schedule, Ursula Hatcher moved about the small enclosure that represented both the first floor of her home and the official U.S. post office for the region encompassing Hades and a hundred-mile radius. This had been the only post office for the area ever since the mail had found its way to Hades more than a hundred years ago.

Her grandfather had been the first postmaster. He'd passed the mantle to his son, her father. Since all three of his sons had left the area before their eighteenth birthday, he allowed his youngest to assume the duties of postmaster, transferring the position to his only daughter. She'd served well these past fifty years. And hoped to make it through another twenty, if not more.

When she passed on, she assumed, hoped really, that the job would be taken over by one of her own, even though they now had different occupations to keep them busy.

She frowned over a letter as she tried to decipher the addressee. She liked to think that, eventually, April or Max or June would hear the calling in their blood and do their duty.

But that day was far away. Just as was her demise.

Making up her mind as to who the letter should go to, Ursula pitched it in its pigeonhole and smiled. She intended, quite frankly, to live forever. Or as close to forever as God saw fit. Finished with the smaller of the two bags, she dragged the other over closer to the bench to continue sorting.

The mail had arrived later than usual. Sydney Kerrigan hadn't been able to get to Anchorage for it until just a little while ago. Her youngest daughter was ill and she'd had to wait until one of her other children was home from school to watch her before she could make the mail run.

The task would be a lot simpler if deliveries came every day instead of every other day or every third as they did in the dead of winter, Ursula thought. She bent down and picked up a handful of letters, beginning the long task of sorting through the new arrivals.

What they needed was a regular transport service. And more planes. They were a growing town now and growing towns had needs beyond restaurants and movie theaters and hotels, all of which had gone up or were going up lately.

They needed a reliable mode of travel and since the roads were impassable for months at a time, that meant airplanes. Something like an air taxi service.

It was something she planned to take up with Kevin Quintano. He'd just sold his old business and had money to burn, according to Jimmy.

She thought of Kevin and smiled. Now there was

a man in search of a reason to exist if she ever saw one. A transport service and her granddaughter should be more than reason enough.

Ursula laughed to herself, the sound approximating the cackle of a hen just after she'd laid an egg.

The cackle faded when the front door opened and then closed quietly.

"If you're here for the mail, I haven't finished sorting it yet so you might as well go on home and come back later. These things can't be rushed," she announced without turning around.

"I'm not here for the mail."

Her hands froze mid-shuffle. The male voice had every muscle in her body stiffening.

There was nothing wrong with her memory. Even if there'd been more than a handful of years since she'd heard that voice.

Setting down some envelopes on the counter, Ursula turned slowly around. And looked into the face of her son-in-law.

The years hadn't been kind to him, she noted. Good. His once-handsome features were dulled and etched with the lines of hardship. There was no joy about him, nor excitement or lust for the open road. She hadn't recognized him.

There'd been a thousand different things she'd planned to say to him if she ever saw him again. But all she could do was sigh. It spoke volumes.

"What are you doing here?"

He met her gaze head-on, though he looked as if he wanted to look away. "I've come to apologize." He took a step forward, then stopped. "I know I can't make amends, but I want to try."

Painful memories assaulted her in waves. She did her best to ignore them, to beat them back. Ursula laced her hands together in front of her. "Rose is dead."

The words seemed to cut into him. He closed his eyes. "I know. I was at her grave today." When he opened them again, tears shimmered there. "Was it painful?"

Crocodile tears, Ursula told herself. "Broken hearts usually are."

It vaguely occurred to her that men who were irretrievably lost at sea probably wore the same desperate look. "Ursula, I—"

She didn't want to hear words that would do no good. The past couldn't be fixed. She was only concerned with the present and whatever future there was before them. She always had been.

She thought of gesturing him toward a chair, then decided that he needed to stand.

"You know, when she first died, I thought about finding you and killing you myself with my bare hands. Tearing your body from limb to limb and scattering the remains from here to Nome." She'd gone over that scenario at great length in her head as she lay awake at night. In the beginning, it was what kept her sane.

Ursula looked up into the face of the man who'd cast such a irreversible spell over her only daughter. The hatred, she discovered, had long since left her heart. A heart given to hate withers and dies and she'd had grandchildren to care for.

"But the truth is, you weren't responsible for Rose's death. She was. I lost three men. All good." She looked at him pointedly. "Better than you, no doubt." She didn't wait for his grunted response. "The trick to life is that you just keep on living it." She picked up the mail again and continued sorting. "Keep on looking for the good in it. Rose had good in her life." Stopping, she peered over her shoulder at her grandchildren's father. "She had three kids who loved and needed her. But she chose to look only at the negative. So, in the end, it wasn't you who did her in—it was her."

She picked up another batch and began to slowly sort through them by route. Since none of her grandchildren had called to tell her that Wayne Yearling was in the area, she assumed that she was his first stop. "This making amends thing, does it include your kids?"

"Yes."

"Good." She nodded, approving. "You *should* try to connect with them. They're still young. They can come around in time, although I wouldn't be holding my breath about any parties being held in your honor real soon.'' This was, she knew, going to take a great deal of time.

The pause behind her was so long she thought he'd left the building. "I'm dying, Ursula. The doctor gave me maybe six months. Maybe a little more."

Her hands were stilled for a moment as she took in this latest curve ball that life was throwing her way. And then she went on sorting briskly.

"We're all dying, Wayne. You just happen to know more or less when. My way of thinking, you've got a jump on the rest of us." She shoved a letter into a space that was already crammed. Gilhooly hadn't come by for his mail in a long time. She wondered if she should be forwarding it somewhere. Tabling the thought for now, she turned around to look at the man who'd managed to drop two bombshells in as many minutes. "To make those amends you mentioned before you have to stand in front of the postmaster general in the sky."

For the first time since he'd entered, there was a trace of a smile on his lips. "Ursula, I don't know what to say to you to—"

"Then don't try," she cut him off. She didn't need or want his apologies. She wanted her son-in-law to move on to the next level. "I've made my peace with all this, Wayne. With you, so to speak. Spend your energy on the others."

The mention of others had his smile fading. "I saw June at the cemetery."

Her mouth curved slightly. June. The fierce one. "I'm surprised you're still standing. She took your leaving and her mother's death just as hard as the others, even though she was just a bit of a thing." Maybe even more so, because she'd been in need of all the nurturing that had to come from different quarters. From her and April and Max.

He seemed to read her thoughts. Despair had Wayne sinking into a chair, his tanned, long fingers knotting before him, like a schoolboy at a loss how to make things right again. "How do I make them understand that I'm sorry?"

That, she knew, wouldn't be easy. "By staying. By not giving up when they turn their backs on you." *And they will, at first,* she thought. He couldn't expect anything less. His expression was so disheartened, she was compelled to say something encouraging to him. "But you're their father. They're so angry because they loved you. Anger's easier to break down than indifference."

Talking wasn't going to change anything right now. Not even his mood. He needed something to keep him busy. She looked down at the mail sack on the floor. "How are you at the alphabet?"

There was a note of hope in his voice, as if her making the suggestion meant that she wanted him to remain. "I know it."

"Good." She pushed the sack in his direction with her foot. The bag toppled. Mail spilled out. "Then come here and make yourself useful."

Eager to make amends, he was quick to comply.

He'd been lying here in bed for the past twenty minutes, holding her to him and feeling her heart beat. He didn't want to let the moment end. But it had to. They couldn't remain like this indefinitely.

He pressed a kiss to the top of her head. They'd made love again and he was absolutely drained. "Still want me to talk to your father for you?"

She wriggled out of bed, reaching for her clothes. "No, I can fight my own battles."

He sat up and scanned the room, looking for his own clothes. "This isn't a battle." He quickly got into his underwear and jeans. He meant to give her privacy as she got dressed, but it was hard averting his eyes. Hard not wanting her again. "From what you've told me, he wants a reconciliation."

She jammed her arms into her shirt as if she were firing a weapon at an unseen target. "What he wants doesn't concern me."

Pushing her hands away, he buttoned her shirt for her, his eyes intent on hers. "June, he's your father."

It was a term that meant nothing in this case. "He's a man who just happened to be there at the moment of conception, that's all. To *be* a father is something else altogether. It means someone who's there, someone who cares.''

He hated to see that kind of hurt in her eyes. Hated knowing what it had to be doing to her inside. ''Just because a man's a father doesn't mean he's automatically strong.''

She dragged her fingers through her hair, untangling it. ''What does strength have to do with it?'' she challenged.

Strength had everything to do with it. When she got older, she'd understand. ''It takes a great deal of strength to stay, to make a life for not just yourself but your family.''

It wasn't as if her father had accidentally made her mother pregnant and moved on. He'd *married* her, had three children with her. He *knew* what he was up against, what he was doing. And she hated him for it. For not loving any of them enough to stay.

''Well, if you can't do it,'' she snapped, ''you shouldn't have a family.''

She was about to storm out of the room. He placed his hands on her shoulders, turning her around to face him. ''Hindsight, June.''

Where was he going with this? ''What do you want me to do, just forgive him?''

''Yes.''

Her mouth dropped open. Though she'd thrown the words at him, she hadn't expected him to actually agree. It took the wind out of her sails. "You really want me to forgive him?"

"Yes."

Anger filled her. Kevin was supposed to be on her side, not her father's. He didn't even know her father. "He doesn't deserve forgiving."

That was beside the point. "Maybe he does, maybe he doesn't, but you deserve not to have to live with this anger consuming you this way."

Where the hell did he get off making judgments like that? Shrugging him away, she squared her shoulders. "You don't even know me—beyond the obvious."

"Yes, I do," he contradicted quietly. "Because what you feel, I've felt. My father didn't have to withdraw the way he did, didn't have to leave me with the responsibility of doing what he couldn't do. We needed him, my brother, my sisters and me, and he just copped out." She opened her mouth and he knew what she was going to say, that it wasn't the same thing. But it was. "He didn't go off whistling with a backpack slung over his shoulder, but he went just the same. And he took most of the dreams I had at the time with him."

She wanted to know about those dreams. But all June could say was, "Then you do understand what I'm feeling."

"Yes. But I also forgave my father. Because not to forgive him made me bitter." He touched her cheek, making her look up at him, trying to make her see. "And bitter is a terrible way to be."

Frustrated, June sighed. "I'll think about it."

"Good." He followed her into the hall. She hurried across the floor like a woman with a purpose. "Where are you going?"

"I've got to go into town." She saw Kevin looking over toward the telephone. "This isn't the kind of thing you do on the phone."

She probably had a point. "All right, I'll go with you."

She didn't need a guardian or a protector. "No, you don't have to."

"Yes," he said quietly, "I do."

Irritated without fully knowing why, she stood her ground. "Just because we made love doesn't mean you own me."

"That has nothing to do with it. You look like you need a friend."

She was going to answer that she didn't need anyone, but that was a lie and they both knew it. Everyone could always use a friend. Her heart warmed. She threw open the front door, then looked at him over her shoulder. "Well, what are you waiting for?"

He followed her across the threshold. "Not a thing."

Chapter Twelve

"You know?"

June stared at her grandmother, dumbfounded. It had taken her several minutes just to work up to the subject of her father's reappearance, afraid that the shock might be too much for the woman. Despite her rigorous protests to the contrary, Ursula's heart was not as rock solid as it had once been.

But instead of shocking her grandmother, the woman had wound up stunning her.

Ursula Hatcher sat complacently behind her desk, presiding over the small government domain that had been hers all these many long years. Her eyes were kind as she looked at her youngest grandchild.

"He was already here."

Obviously all her worrying about the state of her grandmother's heart had been pointless. The woman appeared to be taking this far better than she was.

"And?" Impatience surrounded the single word.

With a great amount of care, Ursula began to re-organize the first-class stamps filed away in her drawer. She kept her eyes on her work. "He said his piece and left—after I put him to work for a while."

The sigh that escaped her granddaughter's lips was just short of being classified as a gale. "Grandma—"

She glanced up as she continued refiling the stamps by age. "I don't throw stones, June." She closed the drawer with finality. "And everybody deserves a sec-ond chance, especially if they're sincere."

Was her grandmother getting naive, or had she al-ways been that way? "He's not sincere."

"Oh, I think he is."

Ursula prided herself on not having wool pulled over her eyes. She'd seen through Wayne Yearling when he'd first come calling on her daughter. And saw him for what he was now. A broken man looking to right at least one wrong before he died. She judged by the way June was carrying on that she didn't know about her father's limited status on this earth.

"Doesn't hurt anything to give it some time." She sat back and looked at the two young people before her. She sensed that Kevin knew what she was talking about. "I couldn't find it in my heart to throw him out. Maybe I could have once," she allowed, "but not now. I don't think Max will either." Ursula paused to think for a moment. "I'm not a hundred percent sure about April." Her words were addressed to Kevin. "She was the oldest and thought she was his favorite."

June laughed shortly, dismissing her grandmother's words. "*He* was his own favorite."

Ursula's voice was calm, considerate. "Don't think that's true now, June-bug."

Kevin raised his eyebrows in amusement as he looked at June. "June-bug?" Somehow, it fit.

Ursula nodded. "Nickname we gave her when she was a little bit of a thing." She shifted her chair to better face him. "June was always exploring, crawling into things and getting stuck."

The grin was so wide it nearly split Kevin's face. "June-bug, huh?"

Her grandmother was the only one allowed to call her that. "Don't even think it," June warned.

Ursula saw this as the perfect opportunity to steer the conversation away from the subject that was so painful to her granddaughter. "Kevin, I hear you're looking to invest your money in something."

Investing made it sound so distant, as if he was going to sit back and let his money do his earning for him. That held absolutely no appeal for him.

"I'm looking for a new business venture." After working on the farmhouse for all this time, he was

acutely aware of things in need of repair. He looked
around the post office. It could use work. "Why, do
you need renovations?"

When Ursula smiled, there was still a great deal of
the young girl who had once captured the hearts of
all the men in the area. "No, but I hear you're pretty
handy at that, too." Her eyes sparkled as they shifted
toward June and then back to him.

June rolled her eyes. When she was younger, there
were times when she thought her grandmother had
built-in radar. Things hadn't changed all that much.
"Meet my grandmother, our answer to the Internet
and a gossip column, all rolled into one."

"It's not gossip if it's true." Ursula pretended to
sniff. Her explanation, again, was for Kevin. "It's a
public service. Otherwise, people might stay in the
dark for months at a time."

"Not hardly." This time, there was a touch of
fondness in June's tone.

Kevin perched on the edge of Ursula's desk.
"What's this business you want me to invest in?" He
had no intention of looking into a business up here.
It was too far away from everything he knew. But
there was no reason, he told himself, not to keep an
open mind.

"We need a transport service." Ursula told him
only what had been on the minds of those who cared
about Hades. "We're growing and we can't always
wait for Sydney or Shayne to fly out to get supplies

for us, or take one of us where we need to go if we haven't got the time to waste with winding roads and wayward bears.

"It's not so bad in the summer," the postmistress allowed, "but winters are a challenge. If someone came here, say brought in a couple more planes and pilots with him, hell—" she snapped her fingers "—he'd see his money just come pouring back in no time. After that, it's gravy." She leaned in to him like a fellow conspirator. "So, what do you say?"

She was putting him on the spot, but he didn't mind. Ursula was like the grandmother he'd never had and he'd become instantly fond of her on their first introduction. "Not shy about things, are you?"

She snorted at the observation. "This is Alaska, boy. If a woman's shy, she winds up frozen on an ice floe somewhere. A woman has to say what's on her mind up here." Her eyes took measure of him. She could see the verdict was undecided, but she was hopeful. "How about it? Are you game to bring flight to the citizens of Hades?"

His first instinct was to say no, but the second one made the possibilities sound at least somewhat intriguing. He was aware that June was moving about the room restlessly. They had to get going. "I'll give it some thought."

Ursula drummed her fingers on her desk, trying to bank down impatience, knowing that, as a logical man, he wouldn't just jump into this the way Yuri might if she suggested it to him.

"Well, don't take too long," she warned. "Wedding's in about a week. I hear your ticket's for the day after."

He laughed out loud. "Is there anything you don't know?"

Her eyes met his. Her tone delved down to the inner workings of his soul, where his secrets lay. "Lots of things, Kevin my boy, lots of things."

Kevin couldn't help the smile that rose to his lips. He hadn't been referred to as a boy since before he'd stopped being one. Even when his parents had been alive, there had been a certain amount of responsibility that had fallen on his shoulders because he was the oldest. He'd assumed it naturally and his parents never attempted to dissuade him, to try to force him to enjoy his boyhood a little while longer.

He missed that now. Missed having carefree memories to look back on.

"You might try talking to the Kellogg boy," Ursula suggested. "He knows how to fly and he used to work for a transport service before he went to work at the emporium. He might give you some information."

Enough was enough. It was time to come to Kevin's rescue. June hooked her arm through his and began to pull him toward the doorway.

"Leave him alone, Grandma. Kevin's not interested in owning a transport service."

He wasn't absolutely sure that was true anymore. Gently he disentangled himself from June. It struck him how very similar she was to her grandmother. And to Lily, for that matter. His sister was going to fit right in here, bossing men around.

"Kevin's got a tongue and can talk for himself, June-bug," he told her pleasantly, anticipating the flare that instantly came into her eyes at the mention of the nickname.

June curbed her tongue. He needed to get a couple of things straight, but she wasn't about to go into them in front of her grandmother.

"I was just trying to get her to back off a little," she told him, casting an accusing eye toward her grandmother. "She can be intense when she wants something."

It was hard not to laugh, listening to the pot call the kettle black. "That kind of thing seems to run in the family."

Ursula took no offense at the comment. Her mind was on more important things. "So—" she leaned forward "—are you interested?"

He thought about it for a moment longer. "I might be. I'm always interested in a good proposition."

Her grandmother looked directly at her when Kevin said that. June tried to remain unfazed, but she had a feeling that color was creeping up into her cheeks anyway. There was laughter in her grandmother's eyes as she turned away.

June grabbed his hand. "C'mon, Kevin, I've got to see if I can find April and Max." Her gaze was somewhat accusing as it shifted to her grandmother for a moment. "Someone has to warn them."

Her grandmother's voice followed them through the door. "I'm sure you'll do a perfectly fine job of that, dear."

June felt utterly drained as she sank down on a chair at her kitchen table.

Not even the music that had greeted her as they walked into the house had heartened her despite the fact that the tune was one of her favorite songs. She was tired and frustrated. It had taken the better part of two hours to track down her siblings.

April was out in the field, taking photographs for a magazine assignment she was currently putting together and Max had been at the Inuit village, trying to quell a dispute over fishing territory. It was a credit to her brother that the Inuit trusted him to come in and arbitrate their disputes, but she hadn't dwelled on how proud she was of him, of both of them for what they'd become.

Her mind was on other things. She'd wanted them solidly behind her in this.

And they weren't.

Max took the news the way he took most things—

stoically. When she'd told him that their father was back, hat in hand, his expression had hardly flinched and barely changed, although he'd smiled a greeting when he'd seen them approaching. He hadn't said how he felt about the reappearance, or the plea for forgiveness.

April had been visibly stunned at the news of their father's sudden return. She hadn't made any quick declarations about the situation either.

Neither had looked the way she felt. Angry, indignant. And it bothered the hell out of her.

Kevin entered the kitchen behind her. He'd let her have her lead all the way back to the farmhouse after they'd seen Max. June had chosen to sink into an almost deafening silence.

It was time for words. Silence, he'd learned years ago, never solved anything but only served to isolate you.

"You wanted them to react the way you did, didn't you?"

Her legs straight out before her, she contemplated the tips of her boots. "Yes," she finally said grudgingly. Was that so unreasonable, to want her brother and sister to feel the way she did? "He left all of us. He broke my mother's heart."

He noted that she'd said "my" not "our." Was it the bond between them that she felt she was now vindicating? Was this a battle for two rather than just one? He decided to take her lead.

For a moment, he dropped down in the chair opposite her, straddling it. "What would your mother have done if she was alive right now?"

The expression on June's face was disparaging. She knew exactly the way her mother would have reacted. "Welcomed him back with open arms, probably."

"Why?" he prodded.

Anger flickered in her eyes as she raised them to his face. "Because she loved him. And because she had no self-pride."

"What if he came back to stay?"

"He didn't," she cut in quickly. Her father never stayed put anywhere. At first, there'd been postcards. There'd been no return addresses on any of them, but the canceled stamps had testified to a wide journey. They'd stopped coming after a year. That eventually had led them to speculate that he had died.

"What if he did?" Kevin pressed. "What if he came back for good? Wouldn't cutting him off like that be cruel to everyone considered? To your mother as well as to him?"

What did he want from her? He was just spinning theories anyway. "I suppose."

"So, why wouldn't that apply here?" he asked gently. June looked up at him, confusion in her eyes. "If your father's come back to Hades to make amends, wouldn't turning your back on him now be just as cruel to him? To you?"

Restless, she got up, nearly knocking her chair

over. Kevin caught it, righting the chair as she shoved her hands irritably into her pockets. "Don't you understand? I can't just forgive him."

"No," he confessed, "I don't understand. Why can't you forgive him? What good does it do to punish him?" And herself, he added silently, sensing how much she was hurting. "It doesn't change anything that's happened. Doesn't bring your mother back. And it only robs you of the present, of the future."

He was talking to her back. Hands on her shoulders, Kevin turned her gently around. When she resisted, he applied just enough pressure to make her look at him. There was a world of hurt, of confusion in her eyes.

"He's here now, June, make the most of it. None of us know how much time we have on this earth. We shouldn't waste it. Enough's been wasted as it is."

She looked away, shaking her head, blinking back tears she refused to shed for her father. "I can't."

"Yes, you can," he told her softly. "You're not a vengeful person."

Her head jerked up. What gave him the right to make these judgments, to act as if he knew the workings of her mind when she didn't know them herself? "How would you know? How would you know anything about me? Two weeks isn't enough time."

He curbed the urge to take her into his arms, to just hold her until her hurt ebbed away. He knew she'd never allow it, not now. "Sometimes two weeks can be a lifetime."

"Only if you're a mosquito." She sighed, shutting her eyes. "I need time, Kevin. I feel my whole life has been based around his leaving us."

"You're working the farm."

She opened her eyes to look at him. "What does that have to do with anything?"

"Aren't you back here, where you lived as a child, to try to change things, to turn things around? To see what it might have been like if you'd all stayed here, trying to make a go of working the land? Of living here instead of with your grandmother above the post office?"

Her denial died on her lips. She supposed he was making sense. Kind of. "Jimmy never told me you were a philosopher."

"He should have." He laughed, remembering. "God knows I spent enough time trying to talk sense into him when he was a teenager."

June leaned back against the ancient counter that ran along the wall. "I'm not a teenager, Kevin," she pointed out.

"Nobody outgrows their need for common sense." He peered out through the kitchen window. Daylight was streaming in full force. But he could feel his stomach tightening. He'd left the watch Luc had lent him on the bureau in his room. He still couldn't find his own.

"Damn it." He turned to look at June. "I can never tell by looking. What time is it?"

She felt she'd packed a great deal of living into this one day. June glanced at her watch. "Almost five, why?"

"I was just thinking that dinnertime will be coming up soon."

The only schedule she adhered to had to do with working. In her personal life, she was far more lax. She ate when she was hungry, slept when she was tired. She pressed her hand to her stomach, remembering that she'd had very little to eat today. "I really don't feel like cooking."

"That wasn't going to be the offer," he told her. "I can either make something for us, or we can go over to Lily's." Never one for pretenses, she was staying with Max at his home. She'd reasoned that since she was going to be living there after the wedding, she might as well get a jump on redecorating it now. Max had seen no reason to argue with her. "She's always game to whip up a meal or twelve."

Even though he'd seemed to take the news well enough, Max was going to need Lily tonight, June thought. And while there was a need within her to band together with her siblings, there was also a desire to be alone. To lick wounds that had been freshly ripped open.

She shook her head at the latter suggestion. "I don't feel like going out again."

It was just as well, he thought. She needed a little time to rebound from this. And, selfishly, he wanted to be with her. "Okay, then I'll cook."

She sighed. "I'm being waspish, short-tempered and surly. Why are you being so nice to me?"

He lifted her chin and looked down into her eyes. His own smiled softly. He thought of the way she'd been earlier, so pliant, so willing in his arms. He might have been her first, but the way he saw it, she had been his salvation.

"It's a dirty job, but someone has to do it." He brushed a kiss against her lips. "Now, why don't you just relax and let me do the work?"

She nodded, then flushed, feeling guilty. She'd had so much planned for today. "I haven't gotten anything accomplished today."

She sounded like him, he thought. Before he'd learned better. "Not every day has to end with a mountain of accomplishments arrived at by exerting muscle power." He opened a cupboard but didn't find what he was looking for. "You've left your mind open to a possible truce. I'd say that was a great deal of work for one day."

June turned to look at him. She'd never met a man like Kevin before. Something stirred within her, but she refused to let it rise. "Did you ever think about putting all these sayings of yours into a book?"

"Another undertaking to consider." He laughed as he continued to hunt for a large frying pan. He'd found one pan, but it was small and hopelessly burned along the bottom.

Two pots fell at his feet as he opened the next cupboard. Apparently her method of putting away cookware was to shove it into a closet and close the door quickly, praying that the laws of gravity would hold it in place.

The laws took a holiday.

With a sigh, knowing she had to do something, June crossed to where he was standing and picked up the fallen pots. She thought of the way her grandmother had badgered him earlier.

"What about that other undertaking?" she asked, leaving the pots on the counter.

Finding what he was looking for, he took the liberty of rinsing the pan out in the sink first, just in case the pots shared space with small, furry creatures. "Which one?"

"The one my grandmother sprang on you. The transport service." Did he want her to spell it out for him? To tell him that even though she'd rescued him from her grandmother's grilling, part of her hoped he'd say yes to the proposition? "You weren't serious when you said you'd think about it, were you? I mean, you were just humoring her, right?"

He dried off his hands on the towel. Unable to read the look in her eyes or to decide which answer she wanted from him, he asked, "Would you want me to be serious?"

Irritation rose. "Why do you always answer a question with another question?"

"It's what we philosophers do." He laughed when he saw her frowning. "You're the one who called me that, not me. I asked the question to find out how you felt about it." He paused before opening her refrigerator, one that he had taken the liberty of stocking on his third day of work. "How would you feel about it?"

The shrug was a little too deliberate, a little too studied. "We could use a transport service," she acknowledged, then built on her words. "Hell, as far as I'm concerned, we're way overdue for one. We could have used it a year ago. Maybe if we had one, I wouldn't have sold my repair shop." When he looked at her quizzically, she added, "A lot of business comes in from fixing planes."

"You can fix planes?" There was no end to the surprises the woman was hiding in her bag of tricks, was there?

"I can fix anything that has to move." She wasn't bragging—it was a simple fact. "With the possible exception of some of the old men at the Salty."

"You had trouble with the tractor," he reminded her, a grin playing on his lips.

She ran her tongue along her lower lip, suddenly wanting to kiss him. To keep from giving in to the whim, she took a step away from him.

"It was just a matter of time," she hedged. "You figured it out first."

He nodded. "I really wasn't talking about how you felt about having a transport service."

"Then what were you talking about?"

"How you felt about me buying one."

She wasn't about to get pinned down. Not when he didn't say anything first. "Someone has to. Might as well be you."

"And that's it?"

Her look was hesitant. Edgy. "Why, what else do you want?"

He smiled indulgently at her. "Now who's answering questions with questions?"

She began to drift around the small area, aimless. She'd never really fit into a kitchen. "I like to think I have an open mind and learn as I go along."

He tried another approach. This was not the outspokenness her grandmother had claimed was the hallmark of women out here. He was pulling teeth. "Would it bother you if I were around?"

"You're family. Why shouldn't you be around?" She pressed her lips together. "Are you thinking about being around?"

He shrugged, afraid to commit himself, especially when she didn't seem to want his commitment. "Maybe."

She nodded slowly. "It's good for the town."

About to slice carrots, he glanced in her direction. "How about for you?"

"Hey, what's good for the town is always good for me."

She took it no further than that.

She had no feelings about it one way or another. He didn't have to be hit on the head to pick up a cue, Kevin thought. He turned his attention back to making supper for them.

Chapter Thirteen

Kevin climbed down off the ladder to survey his work. His mind wasn't really on the wall he was painting, except in the most perfunctory of ways.

They'd been steering clear of each other.

Not an easy matter since he was still coming over to work on the house.

Having finished the exterior, he was now busy painting the rooms themselves. Because June hadn't expressed a preference for any particular color, he'd made the decision for her. He'd painted the walls a light shade of icy-blue, using white as an accent whenever he could. The house was slowly going from oppressively dreary to bright and cheery.

The same couldn't be said of their relationship. Whatever conversation might have existed before had now disintegrated into short sentences populated with fleeting, monosyllabic words. Not wanting to press, he'd taken his cue from her, thinking that June had either decided to regret what had happened between them or was trying to work her way through her ambivalent feelings regarding her father's appearance and Yearling's desire to make amends any way possible.

In any case, she was reacting to Kevin as if he were some kind of stranger, not a man she'd made love with. He wasn't sure just how much more he could take in tolerant silence.

June was gone more than she was there. She was either working in the field, working in the barn or going to town to talk to her relatives.

The one thing that was clear was that she didn't want any part of him.

It put a whole new light on things for him as to his thoughts about actually relocating here and starting up a transport service for Hades. As he'd mulled it over, the latter actually began to sound like a good idea in his opinion.

But his motives weren't so grounded in rock.

With a sigh, he retired his paintbrush, leaving it horizontally perched across the mouth of the paint can. Initially, the idea of investing his time and money in a business here had to do with being close to his family. Lily had been gone from Seattle only a short while, and although they hadn't exactly lived in each other's pockets, they had gotten together a couple of times a week. He would either come to her restaurant, or Lily would drop by the house. The fact that lately the only time he heard her voice, or any of their voices, was when he picked up a telephone to call didn't really sit well with him. He was and always had been, first and foremost, a visual person. Sight figured in quite prominently with his required family hit. That meant relocating here.

But if he were being honest with himself, the real reason he'd begun to explore this business possibility was June. Running a transport service would give him a good excuse to interact with her. After all, the planes were going to need a regular mechanic and June didn't seem completely wedded to the idea of the farm. Oh, she was working hard at it for the moment, but he suspected that was because it wasn't in her to do anything else, even if she wasn't really committed to the idea of making farming her calling. June wasn't a woman who believed in half-measures.

Woman.

His mouth curved in a smile tinged with surprise as well as a bittersweet feeling. That was the first time he'd referred to her as a woman, not a girl, in his mind. Maybe he was losing his grasp on the age thing as a stumbling block.

Heaven knows he certainly couldn't think of her as

a girl anymore. Not after the other day. First time or not, she'd been all woman in his arms.

And he ached for her.

He wiped his hands on the cloth that was hanging from his back pocket. Without the protective shield of ageism to hide behind, it hit him with the speed of a bolt of lightning. June was, quite frankly, everything he'd ever wanted in a woman.

In bed and out.

But it was the out of bed that was now the problem.

Age might not be a factor, but there were other things in the way now. Predominantly the barriers she was throwing up between them. Maybe he'd been too convincing in his initial arguments about being too old for her and she'd finally decided to believe him.

Or maybe there were other demons she was wrestling with.

In either event, he had to decide whether to remain here and try to make her come around, or just leave her be and accept the fact that maybe this was one of those things that wasn't meant to happen.

He sighed, wadding the cloth up and pushing it back into his pocket. June had been right about one thing. He did have a tendency to overthink things.

Surveying the room slowly to see if he'd missed any spots, Kevin decided that he was finished with the living room. Time to call it a day. He'd already done the two bedrooms earlier this week. That only left the kitchen, but that could be for another time.

Right now, he wanted to get a little more information about the costs of running the kind of venture he'd been toying with. If it turned out to be prohibitive, that could call a halt to his planning right there. He only had as much money to work with as he'd made by selling the taxi service.

There were other ventures, of course, other things he might be able to do here, but maybe that was just pushing things that weren't meant to be pushed.

Pulling off the T-shirt he'd put on before beginning to paint, he slipped on his regular shirt and headed out the door.

"Have you decided to start that transport service yet?" Max uttered the question by way of a greeting as he stopped by the sheriff's office later that afternoon.

Kevin took the seat he indicated on the opposite side of the desk. "I guess I shouldn't be surprised that you know about that."

"Know about it?" Max laughed. "People haven't been talking about anything else since the subject came up." Thanks to his grandmother, he added silently. "They've taken to thinking of you as their second messiah. You'd be opening up a whole new world to them," he added frankly. There were still citizens, although not too many, who had lived their entire lives within the confines of Hades, never having even ventured out to sample what the rest of the state, much less the country, had to offer.

Kevin didn't want people getting ahead of themselves, especially since he was still very much on the fence about the project. "This is only in the planning stage."

"Most people are hoping you're planning on doing it." Max stopped rocking back in his chair and leaned forward, peering at his future brother-in-law's face. "You are, aren't you?"

"I don't know yet. I like having all the information in before I decide to make a move."

There was a lot to be said for that method. And even more for flying by the seat of your pants, Max thought. He turned to the small desk against the wall behind him and poured two glasses of lemonade.

"That kind of thing might make a man move slower than molasses," Max pointed out. He looked into the older man's eyes. "Sometimes you can't wait for all the information, because it doesn't always come in. Sometimes, you've got to make a move without it."

The conversation seemed to be taking place on several levels. "Are we still talking about planes?"

Max moved the glass of lemonade toward his guest. "We could be." He raised his eyes to Kevin's. "We could also be talking about other things."

Kevin took a long drag of his drink, not realizing how thirsty he was until he'd started. "June?"

Max inclined his head. "Among other things, yes. I'll be the first one to tell you that she's a handful and she's got this one mood she gets into that makes storm clouds look cheery, but those she loves, she loves fiercely and she's got a good heart."

He'd already sensed that about her. That and more. "You don't have to sell me on her."

Max studied his face. There was something going on, something he didn't quite have a handle on. "Then what *do* I have to sell you on?"

"Why would you want to sell me on anything?"

"Because I like you, Kevin," Max told him quite simply. "Because you're family in more than just the legal sense of the word. And because Hades needs good people like you." He paused, studying the bottom of his glass, knowing his younger sister would kill him for this next part if she'd overheard him. "And because June needs a good man."

He was flattered. At the same time, he wished that this wasn't a group operation. What went on between him and June, or didn't go on, was strictly his business. His and June's. "Don't you think it's up to her to decide about that?"

Not being in the middle of a relationship allowed Max to see things more clearly than either of the two participants. He'd already learned that from his own affair with Lily.

"The way I see it—" he wiped away the sweat ring the glass had formed on his desk "—she has.

This thing with our father showing up has thrown her for a loop, thrown all of us, really,'' he amended, ''but more so June because she was the one most deprived of our mother after she died. June adored our mother, and to be shut out that way wounded her more than any of us suspected. Somebody's got to see to the scars, to helping them finally heal.'' He grinned slightly as he looked up at Kevin. ''I hear you've got some medical training.''

Kevin shook his head. ''Only what I've picked up in books. Jimmy's the doctor in the family,'' he reminded Max.

''Which he wouldn't have been if you hadn't put yourself out there for him. And for Alison and Lily.'' Max folded his hands before him as he looked intently at Kevin. ''I know exactly the kind of man you are, Kevin. Your reputation, thanks to your brother and sisters, came here long before you did. You're the kind of man June needs. Don't give up on her.''

That said, he switched topics as he leaned back, nursing the lemonade. ''Have you talked to the Kellogg boy yet? He worked for Trans-state before he came back here.''

Grateful for the shift, Kevin nodded. ''I saw him and talked to Shayne and Sydney just to get a feel for all this.''

''And?'' He must have arrived at some kind of conclusions, Max thought.

Nothing had changed from the time he'd walked

in. "And I'm still thinking. I need to get a few ball-park figures going before I move on to the next step."

Max nodded. He supposed that was only reasonable. It wasn't so much the transport service that he was concerned with, although that would be, in and of itself, a good thing. It was having Kevin committed to something that forced him to remain here.

"Take all the time you need—as long as you come up with the right answer."

The phone rang just then. Max set aside his glass. "I'm going to have to take this."

Kevin was already on his feet. "And I've got to get going, anyway. See you in church." There was a rehearsal set for tomorrow night. The wedding was on Saturday.

That didn't leave much time to make up his mind he thought as he left the sheriff's office.

Finishing up early, her conscience nagging at her, June aimed her vehicle back toward the house, hoping to catch Kevin before he left.

She'd been horrible to him these past few days and he didn't deserve it. But she'd been so confused inside. Having her father turn up this way had brought it all back to her.

The pain, the sorrow. The determination.

She'd sworn to herself that she was never going to be like her mother. She was never going to give any man the power of life and death over her heart. Never be weak.

She was going to be strong. Like April.

But April had found someone, a good someone, and gotten married. And, from all she could glean, her older sister was incredibly happy. Happier than she'd been before she'd married Jimmy.

Her grandmother never seemed to be without some kind of male companionship, not in all the years she could remember. She was pretty sure that the woman was going to wind up letting Yuri wear her down and agree to marry him. All of her marriages, according to Ursula Hatcher, had been on her terms and much too short, cut down in their prime by acts of providence.

Two happy women versus a woman who had lost her heart, her mind and her will to live because she'd loved the wrong man.

How do you know when the right man comes along? Her mother had thought her father was the right man and she'd been horribly wrong.

Approaching the house, she saw that Kevin's car was gone. A sadness swept over her. She felt as if she was driving the last few yards in slow motion, without a purpose.

What did she expect? She hadn't exactly been the Wicked Witch of the West toward him, but no one was going to see him rushing to stuff the ballot box to nominate her as Miss Congeniality, either.

With a sigh, she got out of the Jeep and walked into the house. The emptiness mingled with the scent of fresh paint, making her stomach tighten in a knot.

She wasn't a coward. Why was she letting the idea of loving someone throw such fear into her?

Damn it, why couldn't she have had a normal childhood? Why couldn't her father have loved her mother enough to stay, instead of leaving and breeding a measure of insecurity into all of them?

The front door opened and closed. She was out of the kitchen in less time than it took for the sound to register in her brain.

Kevin.

The knot loosened. A smile climbed up from the center of her being until it adorned her face and lit up her eyes. She could feel it forging a path.

"I didn't expect you back."

He was surprised to find her here. She usually didn't get back until later. "I didn't expect to be back." Kevin scanned the room and saw what he was looking for. Moving around her, he crossed to the scarred, wobbly piece of furniture that served as a coffee table. "I forgot my wallet."

She smiled almost shyly. "Good thing you weren't pulled over for speeding."

Kevin paused after he slipped his wallet into his pocket. Signals were coming at him he wasn't sure what to do with. "That's the first smile I've seen on you all week."

Another man would have been sarcastic. What the hell was the matter with her, running from someone like Kevin? "I'm sorry, I've had a lot to think about." She flushed, finding her way through the field of land mines, otherwise known as an apology. "I know I haven't been very good company lately."

"You haven't been any company lately." Not the kind to dwell on offenses, he offered her an easy out if she wanted it. "I've seen you maybe a total of fifteen minutes since I made dinner for us the other night. I know I'm not as good as Lily, but I'm not bad enough to scare you off that way."

"No." She pressed her lips together, feeling more awkward, more exposed that she was accustomed to. "You're not."

He peered at her face, trying to read between the lines. "But I did scare you off."

She hated the word when it was applied to her. She was supposed to be fearless. The term mocked her. Supposed to be. "What?"

"You didn't contact me," he pointed out. "I scared you off." Maybe he had moved too fast that day. She'd come home, literally shaken and vulnerable, and what had he done? He'd made love with her and probably compounded her problem. "Look, June, I never meant to hurt you—"

"Hurt me?" Now he really had lost her. "What are you talking about?"

"If I'd known that you hadn't—"

She suddenly realized what he was trying to say. "You think I've been acting like such a jerk because we made love?"

"I wouldn't exactly say jerk—"

She cut him off, laughing shortly. "Call a spade a spade, Kevin. We do up here. I've been in a really bad mood and it's because—" It was hard for her to lay her soul bare, even to someone she cared about. "Because I don't know if I'm coming or going right now."

He'd missed her, he thought, missed her the way plants missed the sun. "Do I get a vote in your direction?"

She could feel that smile taking root again. "That depends."

Kevin tilted her head up, to look into her face. "On what?"

"On whether it's the right one." She wasn't the kind who asked for anything, afraid that it would someday come back to bite her. But this was Kevin. Kevin, who opened up a whole myriad of feelings inside her that she had never felt before. Kevin who was good and kind and not a thing like her father. "If I asked you to hold me, would that be very offensive to you?"

"Offensive?" Of all the words she could have used, that was the least likely to match what was going on inside him right now. "Pleasurable, yes. But offensive?" He shook his head slowly, his eyes holding hers. "No, can't say that's the feeling that would be going through me."

The moment his arms closed around her, June felt she'd come home again.

The next step came naturally. He lowered his head and kissed her.

Her body heated immediately. Everything she'd been wrestling with these past few days—her situation, her feelings about her father, about Kevin—all of that faded into the background. Elbowed quickly out of the way by the urgent needs that were suddenly running rampant through her, as if they'd been hovering in the wings, waiting for the first sign of weakness within her.

But this wasn't weakness, it couldn't be. Because even though her knees felt like dampened cotton balls, the rest of her experienced an incredible surge of power flowing through her.

Her breath grew short in her lungs as anticipation took hold. She couldn't wait to rid herself of the cumbersome barrier of clothing that kept her from him.

Kept him from her.

Her fingers felt as if they were getting in each other's way. Buttons refused to leave their holes. She suddenly felt clumsy.

"Hey, steady," he laughed softly, staying her hands as they began tearing away at her clothes.

"Are you laughing at me?"

There was hurt in her voice. "Enjoying you, loving

you, but never laughing, June, never laughing," he assured her.

His lips glided along her face, her throat, making her ache inside. A wildness that hadn't been there the first time threatened to leap out of her veins.

"Let me," he urged softly.

His words barely registered on the edge of her consciousness. And then she felt his hands on her, peeling away her clothing. Peeling away the thin fabric of any resolve that might have been lingering, getting in the way.

He was right.

This was better. Much better. His undressing her heightened the anticipation that poured through her, making it fill every inch of space within her.

She returned the favor, mimicking his movements, spreading her palms out along his chest, his taut belly, dipping her fingers beneath his waistband before undertaking the final step of drawing his jeans away from his body.

Kevin could feel blood pounding through his body, echoing the drumming of his heartbeat. He threaded his hands through her hair, wrapping his fingers through the silky strands. "You pick up things quickly."

"I always have," she murmured against his mouth.

They never made it to the bedroom.

With the strong scent of paint still lingering all around them, they found a haven right there beside the scarred coffee table, on the throw rug that Max had given her as a housewarming gift.

She could feel the imprint of the weave pressing itself into her bare flesh as she moved in a rhythm that Kevin created for her.

The rug crumpled beneath her fingers as she clutched at it, absorbing the sensation of Kevin's mouth as it wove a moist path along her body. Leaving none of her untouched.

Reducing her to a mass of palpitating ashes.

She was barely conscious of sweeping her fingertips along his bare body as he did impossible things to her, evoked impossible responses.

It was even better than the last time.

How was it possible to improve on perfection?

She didn't have an answer to that, but he was doing it. Making her crazy. Making her glow. Robbing her of the chance to turn the tables on him because she hadn't the strength to turn over a match, much less her own body in order to straddle him.

She could only give herself to him and reap in the pleasure from the act.

Over and over again, he'd taken her to the edge and then teasingly, dramatically, pushed her over until she was certain that she couldn't register another feeling, another climax.

But she was wrong.

He came to her. His eyes were filled with an emotion she hadn't seen before, one that made her feel daring and safe at the same time. She arched her hips toward him, borrowing strength from some bank in oblivion.

When he entered her this time, there was no pain. There was only comfort. And unspeakable joy.

It echoed in the way she gasped his name as she sealed her body to his.

And silently gave him her heart.

Chapter Fourteen

Max gave up fumbling with the bow tie that refused to come together and surrendered himself to Jimmy, who had far more experience with this kind of accessory. The last time he remembered wearing a tie, it had been at his mother's funeral. His grandmother had done the honors with it then.

There was a war going on in his gut and he found it difficult not to fidget.

Max looked at his brother-in-law. "Is it natural to want to throw up just before you make the woman you love your wife?"

Jimmy's laugh echoed of kindred feelings held not too long ago when he had been the one taking vows. "Absolutely."

"Look at this." Max held his right hand out to show Kevin while the other men in the small church vestibule looked on in sympathy. "It's shaking."

Kevin nodded solemnly. "That it is."

"It never shook before. *I* never shook before." The feeling in his gut was getting worse. He looked at the men who were his ushers—Ike, Luc and Jimmy—for solace. Or a way out.

"You've never been married before," Ike pointed out. He slipped his arm over Max's shoulders in a moment of intense brotherhood. "Whole different set of circumstances than facing down a measly bear or going after bad guys, my friend." He winked at their heretofore fearless sheriff. "Scarier, too."

Scared wasn't the way to be. Max's fingers hovered over the newly joined bow tie. "Maybe this isn't such a good idea."

Jimmy pushed his hand away before he could do any damage to the handiwork.

"It's a great idea," Luc told him honestly. "Because as scary as the idea of marriage might be, the rewards aren't the kind you can begin to put into words." He smiled his encouragement. "Trust me, my friend, you *want* to do this." He looked at Ike and Jimmy reprovingly. "Don't let any of these idiots play with your mind. None of them would do things any differently, would you?" He paused, waiting. After a beat, Jimmy and Ike added their agreement to his statement.

In an odd way, Kevin didn't feel left out. Granted, he wasn't married like they were, or getting married like Max, but he looked upon these men as family and he felt close to all of them. The realization made him start to think that perhaps there really was something to living in a small community like Hades. Everyone *did* feel they had to look out for everyone else.

"I can't speak for marriage, Max, just for Lily. I've seen her in good times and bad and I've never seen her like this. She's really happy, and Jimmy and I know if Lily's happy, you're going to be happy. Very happy," he emphasized.

Jimmy leaned forward and said in a stage whisper, "You might try remembering that the next time there's an argument on the table."

"Gentlemen?"

Kevin glanced toward the door to see Reverend Hollis peering at them over the tops of small rimless glasses. Cherubic, with thinning hair and kind eyes, he had an ageless quality to him that made him seem young and old at the same time. The minister's warm brown eyes swept from one man to the other before they came to rest on Max. Sympathy immediately flooded his face.

"Oh my, I don't think I've ever seen that shade of white before, outside of a snowstorm." He took a step into the crowded room that was meant for a maximum of three occupants. "Do you want some water, Sheriff?"

Max squared his shoulders. His moment of weakness was passing. "No, what I want is to get through this ceremony."

Reverend Hollis smiled knowingly. This was far from his first wedding. "Then follow me."

Kevin made sure he walked behind Max, in case the latter had any last-minute thoughts about making a break for freedom.

"He looks happy. Doesn't Max look happy?" June asked, hugging his arm to her as they sat at the table reserved for the wedding party.

Kevin waved away a mosquito that was debating having him for a snack. Because Lily's restaurant was still in the planning stage and the weather was mild, the wedding reception was being held outdoors directly behind Jimmy and April's house and within the reach of amenities. Sydney, Marta, Ike's wife, and Ike were handling the meals, threatening Lily with bodily harm if she tried to prepare even one thing. Ike had offered them the use of the Salty, but the saloon wasn't able to hold everyone at once. Besides, Max had decided that he liked the bright sunlight blessing his union better.

It was the one input he'd actually made in the wedding plans, other than selecting his ushers. He hadn't minded being the silent one in this venture, he'd confided to Kevin. He liked seeing Lily happy and she seemed to be in her element, arranging the wedding. Wise man, Kevin thought now, watching Max and his sister as they danced together for the first time as a married couple. They looked stunning together and he couldn't have been happier for both of them.

Kevin nodded. "Yes, he does."

June thought she was literally beaming. "I never thought I'd see the day he got married." She also didn't think that Max could dance like that. Someone must have taken him aside and given him a few pointers. In her heart, she had a feeling that was something that Kevin would do. Always taking care of details and never taking any of the credit. "Max didn't seem to need things like that."

"Like what?"

"Steady companionship. Wife, home, hearth. He was always so self-contained." She turned to look at him, wondering what this emotion was that flooded through her. Maybe she had an inkling as to its identity. "I guess it just takes the right woman to change a man."

The way she could have changed him, Kevin thought. If he were selfish enough to try to claim her. But he wasn't. He had to remember that.

It wasn't easy.

"Works both ways," he commented, looking back at the couple. "Lily's a workaholic. She never let herself have time for relationships."

June frowned. That didn't jibe with what she knew. "I thought she came up here because she broke her engagement and wanted to get over it."

Kevin snorted, thinking of the man who had almost become his brother-in-law. The man was a narcissistic womanizer and he had no idea how someone as sharp as Lily hadn't seen through him from the very first.

"That engagement was meant to be broken. She only hooked up with that character because the rest of us told her she needed to take some time out to relax and enjoy herself. Lily's response was that she already *was* enjoying herself. Then she showed up with that slime on her arm to prove it." He shook his head, remembering. "Lily doesn't like people thinking they know better than she does—about anything."

Kevin glanced at the young woman at his side. She was wearing one of the bridesmaid dresses, a light blue, gauzy affair that made him think of a Grecian high priestess. It was draped so that it accented her tiny waist and made him ache to hold her. When he'd first seen her this morning at the church, he'd almost swallowed his tongue. He realized it was the first time he recalled seeing her in anything other than blue jeans.

She created one hell of an impression in a dress.

He grinned at her. "A lot of that going on these days."

She knew he was referring to her, but she'd never

thought of herself as being stubborn. Only in having the courage of her convictions.

June pretended to sniff. "I don't know what you're talking about." He saw her eyes light up. "Oh look, they're letting the rest of the guests on the floor."

As he turned, he saw that couples were beginning to join Max and Lily. The floor seemed to be holding up pretty well, Kevin noted with satisfaction. It had been quickly constructed just this past week by some of the men in town. He'd put in a couple of hours on it himself, in between working on June's house.

He rose to his feet, taking June's hand. "Well, might as well test out my handiwork."

"You do turn a woman's head," June laughed as she got up from the table.

Nodding at the happy couple, June lay her head against Kevin's shoulder and gave herself up to the music, to the emotions that were slipping through her. It felt like heaven, she thought, dancing with him this way. Pretending, just for a moment, that this was actually their wedding.

She lifted her head to look at him. Maybe someday.

Kevin looked down at her and saw the expression on her face. "What?"

She cocked her head, confused. She hadn't said anything to him. "What 'what?'"

He grinned at her. "You've got a very strange look in your eye."

She lifted her chin slightly, but for once it wasn't

pugnaciously. She was stalling for time, looking for a plausible explanation. She couldn't very well tell him she was thinking about their wedding. Fastest way to send a man running. "Do I?"

A fondness filtered through him. He would have been content to go on dancing like this forever. "Yes."

She shrugged, trying to make the gesture seem casual. "Just thinking."

"About?" he prodded.

"Lots of things." Mischief entered her eyes. "How I'm going to harvest all that wheat, for instance." She looked at him pointedly. "Know where I can find a farm hand?"

Was she asking him to stay? Or just flirting with him? He couldn't decide. He only knew what he wanted it to be. But wishing didn't make it so.

Suddenly he felt her freeze. A startled look entered her eyes. "June?"

"He's here." Her voice was deathly quiet as she stared at someone over his shoulder.

Kevin didn't have to turn to look. He knew she was referring to her father. Max had invited the older Yearling to the wedding after all. The two had made their peace with each other. So had April after a bit. Both had acknowledged that hatred was a terrible thing to harbor and neither one of them had wanted it to continue tainting their lives.

His eyes remained on June's face. "I know."

She looked at him, dumbstruck. "You know?" How could he have known and not told her? Feelings of betrayal immediately sprang up inside her.

Kevin nodded. "Max told me he was inviting him."

All the happiness she'd just been feeling faded into the background. "How could Max not tell me he was doing this?"

"Because I told him not to." Her eyes shifted to him. He couldn't begin to fathom the look he saw there. "Max wanted you to be here and I didn't think he should have to choose between you and his father on his wedding day."

Who the hell did he think he was, making decisions like that? Manipulating her like that? Who the hell did both of them think they were? Her temper flared, rising to a dangerous level.

"We're leaving."

But as she tried to pull away, she found that she was held fast in the same arms that had felt so protective to her only moments ago. He wasn't letting her walk off the dance floor. "We're not going to cause a scene at Max and Lily's wedding."

This time, when she lifted her chin, he saw the old, defensive June materialize. "All right, you stay. I'm leaving."

"No," he told her quietly, still holding her fast, "you're not." He could see that she was inches away from telling him where he could go. His passage to warmer climates didn't matter, but she and what she was feeling, did. "You're going to make your peace with this man, because if you don't, when he dies, you'll never forgive yourself."

Her eyes narrowed. "What do you mean, when he dies?"

It wasn't his place to tell her what Ursula had shared with him. That was between June and her father. It was up to Yearling to tell her that he was failing.

"Everyone dies, June," he told her quietly. "Usually sooner than we want them to. Don't leave things the way they are now. The dead might hear us when we ask for forgiveness, but we can't see them hear us. And it makes a world of difference, believe me. You're bigger than your anger." He lowered his lips to her ear as they continued dancing. "I know you are. Max and April have forgiven him. So has Ursula." He looked at her pointedly.

She didn't want this responsibility. But he was right. And she knew it.

"Damn you," June murmured. Disentangling herself, she walked away from him.

Kevin stood and watched her, knowing in his heart that she wasn't running off the dance floor. Or running at all anymore.

Her slim shoulders braced, she crossed the newly stained, polished wooden floor, her heels clicking in her ears with each step. She walked until she came up to the man who had given her life and taken away her young dreams.

It felt like the longest walk of her life.

Her nerves were vibrating within her as she looked up into his gaunt face. "Would you like to dance?"

For a moment, time seemed to stop. The music continued playing, but it was hardly audible to her as she waited for her father's response.

And then a smile rose to his lips, erasing more than fifteen years from his face. June saw the man her mother had loved with all her fragile heart.

"Very much."

He took her hand in his leathery fingers and led her away from the others. Very slowly, he began to dance to the music.

She was hardly aware of moving. Only of the man who held her to him. He glided on the floor like mist. She looked up into his face. "Mother told me you were a very good dancer."

"It was my partner who was the good dancer. She always made me look good." Wayne's eyes filled with tears. "She was a wonderful woman and I didn't deserve her. We do things when we're young—foolish, thoughtless things that we would never do if we only knew the consequences." He looked at her. "June, if I could do it all over again—"

She nodded. He didn't have to say it, didn't have to bare his pain. Not anymore. She understood. And forgave. "I know, Daddy, I know."

She laid her head against his shoulder as they danced, hiding the tears that came to her own eyes.

The applause that came at the end of the number was as much for her and her father as it was for the musicians who had played the song.

She stepped back to look at her father. The years had been as unkind to him as the lack of him had been to her. "Are you staying in Hades?"

He nodded, obviously pleased that she asked. "For as long as God lets me."

He didn't say for as long as he could, June noted, which would have meant that he'd allow his wanderlust to take him away when the time came. It looked as if his wanderlust was finally gone.

She smiled and hugged him. "Welcome home, then."

Max looked on, feeling a sense of pride, a sense of accomplishment at the reunion, although, he judged, June would have probably come around eventually. She was too kind at heart not to.

Still, he had to admit, albeit silently, that it felt good having had a hand in getting her together with her father.

The band began to play again. It was time to reclaim her. Putting his drink down, Kevin started to cross the floor to where June stood.

But Alan Simpson beat him to it. The tall, lanky miner with the ready smile and shock of blond hair that kept falling into his eyes beat out several other

men as well, all of whom appeared to have the same
goal in mind. Kevin looked around the area immediately surrounding June. All the men looked as if
they wanted to dance with her. He couldn't blame
them. Couldn't blame her for agreeing, either.

The men that were now vying for her attention
were all young, all close to her age from what he
could see. And all very taken with the way she looked
in that bridesmaid dress Lily had selected.

He felt a surge of jealousy even as he picked up
his drink again. No point in being jealous. He'd
known it was going to be this way all along. If he
thought anything else, he'd just been fooling himself.

Kevin took a long sip of his drink, draining the
glass. He debated going in search of another.

"What are you doing all the way over here by
yourself, big brother?"

He turned around to see that Alison was standing
behind him. Her expression told him that she already
had the answer to her question, but was intent on
getting it out of him nonetheless.

He gave her his standard reply. "Observing."

She blew out a dismissive breath. "You do entirely
too much of that, you know."

He smiled fondly at her. He'd missed her nagging,
he thought. "How do you think I got to be so wise?
By observing."

It was an excuse and they all knew that. It was
what he said when he didn't want to get caught up in

things. "It's also how you got to be so isolated." She waved a hand in June's direction. The latter was dancing with Alan Simpson. "Go and rescue her."

Kevin saw the smile on June's face and envied Alan more than he wanted to admit. "She doesn't look like she needs rescuing."

"You don't know the woman like I do." She gave Kevin a small shove, but he remained exactly where he was. She sighed. "I see you haven't gotten any less stubborn since I moved up here."

He arched one eyebrow as he looked down at her. "Neither have you."

"Hey," she laughed, not bothering to deny his assessment, "I had a great teacher." She tried another tack. "Okay, dance with me, then."

"Where's your husband?" Kevin looked around for Luc to come to *his* rescue.

She pointed toward the band. "Over there, spelling one of the musicians."

Luc was picking away at a banjo and looked as if he was having the time of his life. "A man of many talents, your husband."

She laughed warmly, a lusty look coming into her eyes. "You don't know the half of it. Now—" she presented her hands to him expectantly "—are you going to dance with me, or are you going to make me stand here like some pathetic wallflower?"

He looked at all the available men milling around. The numbers here were always in favor of the women, but he welcomed the chance to be with his sister. After tomorrow, he didn't know when he'd be returning to Hades. Though his heart was here, it would be best for all concerned, he decided, if the rest of him was back in Seattle.

Given half a chance, he was sure that more than a dozen men would come scrambling over to fill his young sister's dance card. "Trust me, Alison, you would never be a wallflower, even if you didn't live in Hades."

Her smile, if not her words, told him she appreciated the compliment. "Less talking, more dancing," she instructed.

The moment Kevin took her into his arms, he could feel her trying to get him to move to the left. And June. He shook his head and laughed. "I know what you're up to."

"Up to?" Her look was sheer innocence. "I'm not up to anything. I'm just dancing."

"In June's direction."

She lifted her eyebrows a degree higher, as if to underscore her guilelessness. "Hey, everyone's got to have a direction. Can I help it if June happens to be in my way?"

Which was another thing. "The woman is not supposed to lead," he reminded her.

She looked up at her brother. "Sometimes the woman has to lead. Especially when the man is being too dumb to take the lead himself."

"Alison—"

They were almost beside the other couple now. Alison leaped to take advantage of the opportunity.

"June, do you mind if I cut in?" She didn't wait for a reply. "Of course you don't." Supplanting the younger woman, she took hold of the miner's hands. "Alan, my husband's determined to show the world what he's learned from those banjo tapes he's been watching. I need a dance partner and my brother's got two left feet. Will you please rescue me?"

She gave Alan no chance for rebuttal, but took charge and led him away.

"You do not have two left feet," June protested good-naturedly as she took Alison's place in Kevin's arms. "Dance with me before one of these rutting young stags gets it in his head that he wants to show off."

He obliged, but not before laughing and shaking his head. It was an entirely different breed of women they had up here in Alaska. "Don't you women ever let a man do the asking around here?"

She looked at him with what he could only term a coy look. "We do if he's not too slow."

Kevin made no comment. Instead, he just continued dancing.

Chapter Fifteen

He'd made his decision.

He was doing the thing he knew he should. He was going home.

The thought, fantasy, he'd been harboring before was just that. A fantasy. A dream, nothing more than a desire to recapture a youth he knew he hadn't been able to have the first time around.

Not that he regretted the life he'd had for a moment. He'd made his choice, raised his siblings and given three fine people to the world. People he loved dearly who loved him back just as much. Wasn't that the very essence of the definition of a family? People you loved who loved you back.

If sometimes he missed the thought of having someone by his side, a partner in all this, well, he had no right to make that someone June.

He'd been her first.

There was no reason to believe that he should be her last. She had her whole life ahead of her. She needed her freedom to sample all that life had to offer. The best thing he could do was to give it to her.

There was no doubt in his mind that the next time he came back up here to Hades, she'd be with someone, perhaps even married. He wasn't sure how he was going to be able to handle that. But he'd have to.

It was just another choice he knew he had to make.

Moving from dresser to suitcase, he glanced toward his brother. Jimmy had been there for the past half hour, trying his best to talk him out of leaving. Jimmy's heart was in the right place.

So was his.

At least in theory.

Funny, he never thought that theories hurt. But they did.

Jimmy sat on the bed, watching his brother as Kevin placed his shirts into the single suitcase he'd brought with him from Seattle. Kevin was the only man he'd ever met who knew how to pack neatly.

He just wished that his brother wasn't doing it right now.

Jimmy frowned, shaking his head. They'd gone

around and around about this, but he still knew he was right and for once in his life, Kevin was wrong.

"I said it before. Kev, I think it's a mistake. So do Alison, April and Luc. We all think you should stay on here."

Kevin's mouth curved. "Nice to know my life's been up for a vote by the town council." He carefully tucked the dress shoes he'd brought for the wedding into the suitcase. "If I stay any longer, I'll get lazy."

Jimmy sighed. "We can always find you something else to fix or paint. Lily's going to need a lot of help with that restaurant."

Kevin raised his eyes to look at his brother. "Lily is going to do just fine once she and Max get back from their honeymoon."

Jimmy's good-natured expression gave way to exasperation. "Yeah, but will you?"

Kevin slipped his can of shaving cream into the top compartment. "I've always done fine."

Biting off an oath, Jimmy stopped Kevin's hand before he could put anything else into the suitcase. This was more important than packing. This was about his brother's life. "That's when you had a lot of things to keep you busy. You don't anymore."

Very gently, he disengaged himself from Jimmy's grasp. "That's why I'm going back. To find something to keep me busy."

On his feet, Jimmy moved quickly and got in front

of Kevin so that he blocked access to the closet. "There's something right here for that."

Patiently Kevin moved around him and reached into the closet for his gray slacks. He didn't want to go into this again, into long explanations of why this was the best thing he could do for June. "We've been through this, Jimmy."

Jimmy was nothing if not resilient. If he couldn't succeed one way, he was going to try another. "I meant the transport service."

Kevin knew that Jimmy thought he'd given up on that idea, but he'd done a great deal of thinking on the subject since he'd gathered his information.

"That's not a dead issue yet," Kevin told him. "If I don't decide to invest in that home security company I was looking into before I came up here, I'll be wiring my money up to Ike and Luc. Become their silent partner, so to speak."

It took Jimmy a moment to absorb this new piece of information, coming out of left field. His intent was to get Kevin to stay to run the business, not wire in money. "Ike and Luc?"

Kevin didn't know why Jimmy looked so surprised. "Why not? The two of them are already behind more than half the new enterprises in Hades." His brother was stalling, Kevin decided, trying to make him miss his flight. "Ike said he'd been thinking about investing in a transport service for a while now. Luc usually backs him up—"

Jimmy held up his hand. "What about a pilot?" He knew that Kevin had a license, that he enjoyed flying when he had the chance. That was what had started the whole idea of his running a transport service to begin with.

Kevin was already ahead of him. "You can advertise for one of those." He smiled patiently at his brother. "Don't need me for that."

Momentarily at the end of his arguments, Jimmy shook his head. "You know, for an easygoing guy, you've got one rock-solid head."

Kevin patted his brother's shoulder, the victor even if he really took no pleasure in it. "Not rock solid, just clear thinking. I had a wonderful time, Jimmy, a wonderful time. But this was a vacation. That's all, just a vacation. It's time for me to get back to reality and my life."

Jimmy huffed. "What makes you think your life's in Seattle?"

"I get my mail there." He saw his brother open his mouth again. He had no more time for this. "You're going to make me late, Jimmy. What's worse, you're going to make me keep Sydney waiting. You know how I feel about that kind of thing."

Being on time had been Kevin's only rigid rule. Anything less was an insult to the people you kept waiting. Jimmy didn't like accepting defeat. "I thought maybe, being here, your feelings had changed."

No, his feelings hadn't changed, Kevin thought. None of his feelings. He struggled against the wave of bittersweetness that threatened to wash over him. Now wasn't the time. He had a plane to catch once Sydney got him to Anchorage.

He returned to his packing. "I'll say goodbye before I leave," he promised.

Desperate, Jimmy fired a direct salvo. "What about June?"

"I said goodbye to her last night," Kevin answered after a beat.

He could have sworn he saw his brother's shoulders stiffen just a shade. "Does she know it was that kind of a goodbye?"

He thought of the kiss they'd shared, the very real temptation he'd struggled with not to follow her into the farmhouse. But one last night with her would have simply weakened his decision. A man was only so strong and no stronger, no matter what he'd like to believe.

"She knew I was leaving the day after the wedding. I figure she put two and two together."

"Too bad you can't," Jimmy muttered rather audibly under his breath as he left the room.

Kevin didn't turn around, even though he was tempted to. Instead, he merely smiled to himself. He appreciated what Jimmy was trying to do, what they were all trying to do. But he couldn't allow that to make him change his mind.

It wouldn't be fair to June and June was all that mattered.

He heard a noise behind him. Jimmy was here for round two. But he wasn't about to step back into the ring. Not if he wanted to get out of here on time. "You might as well save your breath, Jimmy. I'm not going to be talked out of it."

"So, you're really leaving."

The sound of her voice, hollow and still, shot through him like a silver-tipped arrow. His breath lodged in his throat as he turned around.

June looked exactly the way she had when he'd first arrived three weeks ago. She was wearing a pair of faded, worn blue jeans and a blue-and-white work shirt over a tank top and rolled up at the sleeves. The perfect farm girl. Making every man who saw her want to suddenly return to the soil and work with his hands.

He hated the accusing look in her eyes, but it was for the best this way. "Yes."

She blew out a slow, measured breath, trying to get a handle on her anger, on her hurt. Just when she thought she knew the man. "I didn't believe it when Alison told me. I thought she'd made a mistake."

Kevin looked away. He had to finish packing. "The plane ticket has today stamped on it."

"And what about you?" She tugged on his sleeve, forcing him look at her. "What do you have stamped on you?"

"What?"

Her temper flared. "Does the word *coward* fit in anywhere?"

It was the anger making her talk that way, Kevin thought. "June—"

But she wouldn't let him speak. "I wouldn't have thought it." Her eyes narrowed. "Not you, not the man who single-handedly raised three kids when he was hardly more than a kid himself. Not the man who told me not to run from life, to leave myself open to things." Her tone grew icy. "But, obviously, I was wrong."

He didn't want it to end like this. Not with her hating him. "Don't you see? I *am* leaving you open to things. To a lot more things than you'd sample being married to me."

Her mouth dropped open. He'd broadsided her. "Married?"

The word had just slipped out. He'd never intended for her to know that he'd considered asking her to marry him. But now that it was on the table, he felt he had to explain. "I'm not the kind of man who'd want to have an affair, June. I'd want to get married."

He made it sound so nebulous. "To just anyone? For the sake of marriage?"

She trapped him in her eyes. "To you. For the sake of happiness. But I've done my living, you—"

Okay, enough was enough. It was time she stopped

being demure and went on the attack. "Have you been to Hawaii?"

He stopped. What did that have to do with anything? "No, but—"

Determined to get her point across, she cut him off again. "Seen the Roman Coliseum?"

"No—"

On a roll, she threw in another location. "Big Ben in London?"

"No." Frustrated, confused, he had no idea where she was going with this. "What are you—?"

She illuminated before he could grope his way around in the dark. "Well, then I guess that makes us about even, because neither have I. We can do those things together if you want." She saw him about to protest. "Or not," she allowed. "Point is, maybe experience equals life, but age doesn't. Someone can do a whole lot of living in ten years, someone else not half that much in a lifetime." She looked at him pointedly. "And I don't have to take a bite out of every chocolate in the box to know which one I want. Now, if you don't want me—"

That wasn't even under consideration. "You know that's not true."

"No." She shook her head adamantly. "I don't. I don't know that because if you wanted me, you'd stay and fight for me—if there was anyone to fight, which there isn't—"

"That miner last night, Alan something—"

She thought for a moment. Except for the wedding itself, and the reconciliation with her father, all she remembered yesterday was Kevin. How handsome he'd looked in his tuxedo. How her heart had pounded when he held her to him and danced.

And then she suddenly realized who he was referring to. "Simpson? What about him?"

"He looked taken with you—"

The laugh almost exploded on her lips. Was that what this was about? He was bowing out for the likes of someone like Simpson? That crazy, wonderful man had it all wrong.

"Alan Simpson would have looked 'taken' with a raccoon if it'd had on a slinky dress." She grew serious, wanting to make herself, her feelings for him, perfectly clear. "And even if he were 'taken' with me, I'm not 'taken' with him." Her eyes looked into his. "What I want is to be taken—by you."

She took a breath, backing away for a moment. The limb she'd climbed out on was fragile and thin and her hold on it was not the best. She fell back on something that was more sturdy, something she felt she could argue successfully.

"What about the transport service? You got a lot of people stirred up about that when you started asking questions, making them think that we were heading into the twenty-first century. Are you just going to give up on that, too? Because if you are, they just might come up with another way for you to leave Hades involving a rail, feathers and some tar.''

Damn it, he wanted nothing more than to take her into his arms again. To tear up his ticket and live out that fantasy he'd allowed himself to buy into. The one that had ''happy ever after'' attached to it. ''They still do that kind of thing?''

She fought against letting the corners of her mouth lift. ''They will if I ask them to.''

His eyes held hers. It was all he could allow himself. ''And why would you do that?''

''To make you think twice about leaving everyone in the lurch.'' She climbed back out on that shaky limb. ''About leaving me in a lurch.''

His heart hurt from wanting her. But she would get over this. All too soon, she'd get over it.

Kevin took her hands in his. ''June, you're caught up in the moment, in seeing your brother get married, in reconciling with your father—''

She almost yanked her hands away, but for once she curbed her temper. Yelling wasn't going to help. She needed to use his best tool against him. Common sense.

''The moment has nothing to do with it, Kevin, except that I want to spend it with you. I want to spend all my moments with you.'' She had to make him understand what he meant to her. It wasn't just the attraction, it was everything. And it would never happen again. ''Look, until you came along, I couldn't see myself ever even thinking of settling down. That kind of thing might have been all well and good for April and Max, but I never wanted to be put into a position where someone else held my heart in his hand. I'd seen what it did to my mother and I swore that wasn't going to be me.''

She smiled at him. ''I guess growing up means that you realize you can't always control what happens to you, or who gets to hold your heart. I figured I got lucky for the first time in my life because the man holding my heart in his hand was good and kind and decent. A man who made me feel safe even while he made me feel other things that I'd never felt before.''

She looked at the suitcase that was opened on the bed. It was packed. All he needed to do was close it and snap the locks down.

''Maybe my luck ran out without me even knowing about it.'' And then she squared her shoulders, looking for all the world like Joan of Arc before she rode into her final battle, a battle she knew she was bound to lose, but bound to fight anyway. ''But even if you don't want me anymore, you can't do this to Hades, can't make them think that you're going to do something for them when you're not. They *need* this transport service, Kevin. On the one hand, the world's getting smaller because of things like the Internet where you can have Mount Rushmore at your fingertips. On the other, here, we're getting more isolated because half the year, we have to rely on Sydney or Shayne to get us places. If you're not going to think about me, at least think about them.''

It was ironic, he thought, that she should choose just those words. Because they were the furthest thing from the truth.

''Not think about you?'' He needed to hold her one more time. Just one more time before he left. Kevin slipped his arms around her, drawing her closer, feeling his pulse come alive. ''Every day of my life for the *rest* of my life, I'm going to think about you. There isn't going to be a waking minute when I won't be thinking about you, about what you're doing and about who you're with.''

Damn it, if he loved her, then why was he leaving? Why couldn't he stay? Did she have to tie him up? ''Wouldn't you rather have the real thing instead of just mental projections?''

Her mouth was so close to his. It took everything he had not to kiss her. ''Yes.''

''Well then?'' She exhaled and her breath lightly slid along his skin. His gut tightened. His desires loosened. She cocked her head, looking for all the world like a cat that had just dined on canary hors d'oeuvres. ''I believe you said something earlier about marriage…''

He held his breath. ''Would you be willing to consider that?''

Restraint wasn't easy. She held back, wanting him to actually phrase the question. Their grandchildren would want to know. "If the right man asked me, yes, I'd be willing to consider that."

Bits of sunshine began to open up within him. "Am I the right man?"

"Kevin, you've always been the right man." Expecting Kevin to kiss her, her mouth fell open as she saw him going down on one knee instead. "Kevin, what are you doing?"

Striking the classic pose, Kevin took her left hand in his. "You've done everything else, I'm going to do this the right way." The smile faded from his lips, to be replaced by a tender expression as he looked up at the woman who held his fate in her small hand. "June Ursula Yearling, will you do me the supreme honor of being my wife?"

Without meaning to, she winced. "You know my middle name."

"Max told me." Now that they were finally at the fateful question, was she having second thoughts? "You're stalling."

Recovering, she grinned wickedly. It was happening, it was really happening. He was asking her to be his wife. "No I'm not. In my book, it's called drawing out the moment—so I can savor it later. And remember it when I want to throw things at you because I'm having a dumb tantrum."

She wasn't going to have tantrums, he thought. Life was going to go smoothly from here on in. "Is that a yes? This has to be official."

"One big, fat yes coming up. Yes!" She threw her arms around him. "Now, do I get to tear up your ticket?"

"No."

"Why?"

He was already making plans. "I'll need it when I go back to sell the house."

She'd half expected that he'd want to keep it, perhaps even have her come there to live. She'd go anywhere, as long as it was with him. But this was the best possible scenario. Because she belonged here. "You're okay with moving up here?"

"Like I told you, everything I've ever wanted is right here." He cupped her face. "Now more than ever."

She couldn't believe one person could feel this happy and still live. "And you won't change your mind?"

"Not a chance."

She searched his face for doubts and found none. "You're sure?"

"I'm sure."

He brought his lips down to hers and proceeded to show her just how sure he was.

Epilogue

"**O**migod, what did you do?"

Lily's horrified demand was directed at the black Labrador retriever Max had given her as a pet when they'd returned from their honeymoon. Behind her came a chorus of gasped exclamations as the rest of June's wedding party filed into the bedroom behind her. It was exactly one hour to the wedding and they'd all gathered there to get dressed.

Except that now June couldn't.

The gangly puppy was standing on what was left of her wedding dress. The rest had become a casualty in an odd tug-of-war between the Lab, King, and his oversize front paws which were firmly planted on the gown, refusing to let it budge while he continued yanking at it with his teeth. There were pieces of white satin everywhere.

June was the last one into the room. As she saw what had caused the others such concern, for the first time in her life, she was rendered utterly speechless.

"Don't panic," April pleaded, looking at her face. "I can run and get my wedding dress."

"Or mine," Lily volunteered. "I haven't packed it away yet. It's in the guest room closet.

"I've still got mine," Alison chimed in. Of all of them, she was the closest in size to June.

The offer was echoed by Marta and Sydney. They all began talking at once to her, afraid of what this latest trauma might do to June. Wedding days were stressful enough without having a Labrador do last-minute alternations on the wedding dress.

June knelt down beside the puppy, who promptly began licking off the makeup Lily had carefully applied to her face.

"Stop, bad dog!" Lily cried, grabbing at King's collar. She pulled the offending animal away. "June, I can't tell you how sorry—"

June waved away her apology. "No, it's all right." Dressed only in lacy undergarments, she sank back on her heels to survey the final damage. There was no saving the gown she had picked out in Anchorage. With a sigh, she looked up at the circle of friends who had closed ranks around her. They all looked slightly panicked. It was strange, but she wasn't. Not anymore. Her life felt as if it was in perfect order and she could cope with anything that came her way.

"No offense, ladies, but there's no sense in rushing out to get any of your wedding gowns." She glanced down at herself. "I'm smaller than any of you."

"With a few pins, we could work miracles," Alison promised, already crossing back to the doorway.

June rose to her feet. "It's going to take more than that—"

"Well, you can't just call off the wedding," April protested.

"Nobody's going to call off anything," Ursula announced as she came into the room, drawn by the commotion. She was wearing a royal purple dress, her favorite color, and looked larger than life as she surveyed the damage done by Lily's pet. She looked at June. "My granddaughter's going to do what she's always done, aren't you, girl?"

"And that is?" Marta wanted to know.

Ursula winked at June as she stooped to pick up the fragments of torn wedding gown. "She's going to rise to the occasion."

All eyes turned to look at the bride.

He wasn't nervous.

Unlike Max before him, and Jimmy before that, Kevin didn't feel that he was about to be separated from his last meal, and he didn't want to make a run for the border. He wanted to be exactly where he was, in the vestibule of the church, about to head for the altar and wait for the one woman in the world he wanted to spend the rest of his life with.

Jimmy could only marvel as he looked at his brother. "God, but you look calm."

Kevin checked the angle of his bow tie in the mirror. "I am calm."

Jimmy pretended to wipe a finger across his brow. He held it up for the others to see. "Look, no sweat. He's telling the truth."

Max peered at Kevin's face. "Aren't you the least bit nervous?"

"No, why should I be?" He smiled complacently. "I've been waiting my whole life for this."

Luc shook his head. "Man's not human."

"No." Ike grinned broadly. "The man knows when he's got a good deal."

"Hey, watch it," Max pretended to take offense. "That's my sister you're talking about."

Ike held his hands up in mock surrender. "Only in the highest sense of the concept, Sheriff."

Jimmy glanced at his watch. It was time. The wedding march would be starting at any moment. "Let's get this show on the road." He gestured for his brother to lead the way.

Kevin couldn't remember when he'd ever been happier. Taking his place at the head of the altar, to the right of the minister, he waited impatiently for the music to begin and for June to make her appearance.

Part of him couldn't believe that this was actually happening, that in less than half an hour the woman who'd won his heart was going to be his wife. It didn't quite feel real to him.

The beginning bars of the wedding march began. A beat later, so did the murmurs.

As one bridesmaid after another made her entrance and walked up the aisle in the company of one of his friends, Kevin felt an uneasiness taking hold. What were the whispers about?

Had someone found a note from June saying that she'd had a change of heart or cold feet or—

And then he saw what had caused the commotion. June was striding down the aisle in time to the music, her arm tucked through her father's. The latter had been beaming with pride ever since June had asked him to be part of the ceremony. It was the best medicine anyone could have prescribed.

But it was June who commanded everyone's attention. Kevin couldn't believe what he was seeing. June was clutching her wedding bouquet and coming toward him. Dressed in blue jeans.

The murmurs in the church increased as speculations were lobbed back and forth amid the pews.

And then somehow, it just seemed right. He didn't care what June was wearing, or not wearing, just as long as she was there.

As Wayne Yearling surrendered June to him, Kevin inclined his head and whispered, "What happened to your wedding dress?"

"The dog ate it," she whispered back. "I didn't want to miss the ceremony. Are you disappointed?"

His eyes caressed her face. "Only if you hadn't shown up."

They turned to face the minister. And to begin a life that Kevin knew was going to be anything but dull.

* * * * *

*If you enjoyed this story, you will love
Marie Ferrarella's new miniseries
from Intimate Moments:*
CAVANAUGH JUSTICE:
*No one is above the law....
Don't miss the first book in this series:*
RACING AGAINST TIME

Available October 2003

It's romantic comedy with a kick
(in a pair of strappy pink heels)!

Introducing

"It's chick-lit with the romance and happily-ever-after ending that Harlequin is known for."
—*USA TODAY* bestselling author Millie Criswell, author of *Staying Single*, October 2003

"Even though our heroine may take a few false steps while finding her way, she does it with wit and humor."
—Dorien Kelly, author of *Do-Over*, November 2003

Launching October 2003.
Make sure you pick one up!

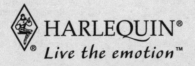

Visit us at www.harlequinflipside.com

✂ **Your opinion is important to us!** Please take a few moments to share your thoughts with us about your experiences with Harlequin and Silhouette books. Your comments will be very useful in ensuring that we deliver books you love to read.
Please take a few minutes to complete the questionnaire, then send it to us at the address below.

Send your completed questionnaires to:
Harlequin/Silhouette Reader Survey, P.O. Box 9046, Buffalo, NY 14269-9046

---

1. As you may know, there are many different lines under the Harlequin and Silhouette brands. Each of the lines is listed below. Please check the box that most represents your reading habit for each line.

Line	Currently read this line	Do not read this line	Not sure if I read this line
Harlequin American Romance	❑	❑	❑
Harlequin Duets	❑	❑	❑
Harlequin Romance	❑	❑	❑
Harlequin Historicals	❑	❑	❑
Harlequin Superromance	❑	❑	❑
Harlequin Intrigue	❑	❑	❑
Harlequin Presents	❑	❑	❑
Harlequin Temptation	❑	❑	❑
Harlequin Blaze	❑	❑	❑
Silhouette Special Edition	❑	❑	❑
Silhouette Romance	❑	❑	❑
Silhouette Intimate Moments	❑	❑	❑
Silhouette Desire	❑	❑	❑

2. Which of the following best describes why you bought *this book?* One answer only, please.

the picture on the cover	❑	the title	❑
the author	❑	the line is one I read often	❑
part of a miniseries	❑	saw an ad in another book	❑
saw an ad in a magazine/newsletter	❑	a friend told me about it	❑
I borrowed/was given this book	❑	other: _____	❑

3. Where did you buy *this book?* One answer only, please.

at Barnes & Noble	❑	at a grocery store	❑
at Waldenbooks	❑	at a drugstore	❑
at Borders	❑	on eHarlequin.com Web site	❑
at another bookstore	❑	from another Web site	❑
at Wal-Mart	❑	Harlequin/Silhouette Reader	❑
at Target	❑	Service/through the mail	
at Kmart	❑	used books from anywhere	❑
at another department store or mass merchandiser	❑	I borrowed/was given this book	❑

4. On average, how many Harlequin and Silhouette books do you buy at one time?

I buy _____ books at one time ❑
I rarely buy a book ❑

MRQ403SSE-1A

5. How many times per month do you shop for any *Harlequin and/or Silhouette* books?
One answer only, please.

1 or more times a week	❏	a few times per year	❏
1 to 3 times per month	❏	less often than once a year	❏
1 to 2 times every 3 months	❏	never	❏

6. When you think of your ideal heroine, which *one* statement describes her the best?
One answer only, please.

She's a woman who is strong-willed	❏	She's a desirable woman	❏
She's a woman who is needed by others	❏	She's a powerful woman	❏
She's a woman who is taken care of	❏	She's a passionate woman	❏
She's an adventurous woman	❏	She's a sensitive woman	❏

7. The following statements describe types or genres of books that you may be
interested in reading. Pick *up to 2 types* of books that you are most interested in.

I like to read about truly romantic relationships	❏
I like to read stories that are sexy romances	❏
I like to read romantic comedies	❏
I like to read a romantic mystery/suspense	❏
I like to read about romantic adventures	❏
I like to read romance stories that involve family	❏
I like to read about a romance in times or places that I have never seen	❏
Other: _____	❏

*The following questions help us to group your answers with those readers who are
similar to you. Your answers will remain confidential.*

8. Please record your year of birth below.

19 _____

9. What is your marital status?

single ❏   married ❏   common-law ❏   widowed ❏
divorced/separated ❏

10. Do you have children 18 years of age or younger currently living at home?

yes ❏   no ❏

11. Which of the following best describes your employment status?

employed full-time or part-time ❏   homemaker ❏   student ❏
retired ❏   unemployed ❏

12. Do you have access to the Internet from either home or work?

yes ❏   no ❏

13. Have you ever visited eHarlequin.com?

yes ❏   no ❏

14. What state do you live in?

_____

15. Are you a member of Harlequin/Silhouette Reader Service?

yes ❏   Account # _____   no ❏   MRQ403SSE-1B

If you enjoyed what you just read,
then we've got an offer you can't resist!

Take 2 bestselling love stories FREE!
Plus get a FREE surprise gift!

Clip this page and mail it to Silhouette Reader Service™

IN U.S.A.	**IN CANADA**
3010 Walden Ave.	P.O. Box 609
P.O. Box 1867	Fort Erie, Ontario
Buffalo, N.Y. 14240-1867	L2A 5X3

YES! Please send me 2 free Silhouette Special Edition® novels and my free surprise gift. After receiving them, if I don't wish to receive anymore, I can return the shipping statement marked cancel. If I don't cancel, I will receive 6 brand-new novels every month, before they're available in stores! In the U.S.A., bill me at the bargain price of $3.99 plus 25¢ shipping and handling per book and applicable sales tax, if any*. In Canada, bill me at the bargain price of $4.74 plus 25¢ shipping and handling per book and applicable taxes**. That's the complete price and a savings of at least 10% off the cover prices—what a great deal! I understand that accepting the 2 free books and gift places me under no obligation ever to buy any books. I can always return a shipment and cancel at any time. Even if I never buy another book from Silhouette, the 2 free books and gift are mine to keep forever.

235 SDN DNUR
335 SDN DNUS

Name	(PLEASE PRINT)	
Address	Apt.#	
City	State/Prov.	Zip/Postal Code

* Terms and prices subject to change without notice. Sales tax applicable in N.Y.
** Canadian residents will be charged applicable provincial taxes and GST.
All orders subject to approval. Offer limited to one per household and not valid to current Silhouette Special Edition® subscribers.
® are registered trademarks of Harlequin Books S.A., used under license.

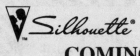

COMING NEXT MONTH

#1567 THE MARRIAGE MEDALLION—Christine Rimmer
Viking Brides

Spirited princess Brit Thorsen traveled far to confront Prince
Eric Greyfell, the one man who may have known her brother's
whereabouts. But Eric recognized the *real* reason fate had sent
Brit to him. She wore the Greyfell marriage medallion plainly
around her neck—marking her as his bride....

#1568 THE RANCHER'S DAUGHTER—Jodi O'Donnell
Montana Mavericks: The Kingsleys

Softhearted Maura Kingsley had a penchant for fix-up projects—
especially when the projects were people! Her latest assignment?
Ash McDonough, the "bad seed" of Rumor, Montana. Ash was
darkly tormented—and incredibly sexy. But good girl Maura wasn't
interested in him. Was she?

#1569 PRACTICE MAKES PREGNANT—Lois Faye Dyer
Manhattan Multiples

Shy, sweet Allison Baker had had one night of impulsive unbridled
passion with attorney Jorge Perez—and she'd ended up pregnant!
Jorge insisted they marry. But theirs would be a marriage of
convenience, not love, despite what Allison's heart wanted to believe!

#1570 SHOULD HAVE BEEN HER CHILD—Stella Bagwell
Men of the West

He hadn't loved her enough to stay. That's what Dr. Victoria Ketchum
believed of her former love Jess Hastings. But Jess was back in
town—with his baby daughter. Could Victoria resist the yearning in
her heart or would temptation lead to a second chance for the reunited
couple?

#1571 SECRETS OF A SMALL TOWN—Patricia Kay

Sabrina March's father's secret had brought her to warm and fun-
loving restaurant owner Gregg Antonelli. But the sins of her parents
kept her from pursuing the heady feelings being with Gregg evoked.
Sabrina's father's legacy of deceit threatened to taint the one love she
had ever known....

#1572 COUNTING ON A COWBOY—Karen Sandler

Single dad Tom Jarret had a problem—his recently suspended nine-
year-old spitfire of a daughter, to be exact. Tom hired stunningly
beautiful teacher Andrea Larson to homeschool his daughter...but
could Andrea's exquisite tenderness teach the jaded rancher how to
love again?

SSECNM0903